PRINCESS BIANCA
AND THE VANDALS

A Post MODERN TALE
OF TWO KINGDOMS

BY NICK LICATA

Limited First Edition of 2,000

PUBLISHED BY FRATRI GRACCHI
705 2nd Avenue Suite 1100
Seattle, WA 98104
www.fratrigracchi.com

COVER & INSIDE ILLUSTRATIONS BY
KAREN LEWIS
karen@jaxom.com

BOOK DESIGN BY KAREN STEICHEN

Printed in the United States of America by
MORRIS PUBLISHING
Kearney, Nebraska

ISBN: 0-9743276-0-3
Library of Congress Control Number: 2003096062

Dedicated to the youth
who protect the earth from those
who would do it harm.

Acknowledgements

I would especially like to thank the following individuals for their help.

Karin McGinn for much guidance and help in editing.

Waverly Fitzgerald, Carol Glickfield, Phyllis Hatfield, Nora Leech, Sher Smith Ross, and Mary K. Whittington for providing very useful review and editing comments.

Laura Vernum, Amelia Iraheta, Nancy Locke, and Terry Brooks for their encouragement and insights.

Nora Leech and E.B. Licata for taking on real adventures and thus prompting me to write this book.

Andrea Okomski for starting me on new adventures.

Sprague Israel Giles for providing me sustenance while I wrote the book.

TABLE OF CONTENTS

PART ONE – THE WIZARD'S MAGIC

PART TWO – JOURNEY TO ZURBIA

PART THREE - SAVING THE FUTURE

PREFACE

In a valley tucked away in one of the far corners of the world, there was a small, forgotten kingdom, innocent but not ignorant of the outside world. By choice they had no cars, trucks, trains, planes or any other kind of machine that used gasoline. The soft mist that hung above their valley all year was as white as goose down. It was a place where time passed slowly, where love and magic were one, and where all the harmful things that had been done to the earth had not been done.

For many years only a few daring travelers would cross the mountains that ringed its valley and descend through its thick forest. Most would stay in the paradise they found. But over time a different kind of visitor would come, not to stay but to plunder. They were the Vandals.

This is a tale of how a young princess had to save her kingdom from the Vandals and a world without magic.

Part One: THE WIZARD'S MAGIC

CHAPTER 1

Suspicions

A shaft of daylight streaked across King Kilian's bedroom and glimmered off the scales of a tightly coiled snake. The Wizard's long, bony hand circled slowly above the reptile's cold, black eyes.

"Never blink when picking up these creatures, it just encourages them to strike," the Wizard said with a devilish smile. The reptile and the Wizard were locked onto each other's gaze. His hand circled ever closer until he slipped it just behind the creature's head. The snake twisted, bared its fangs and hissed as he lifted it. Like a pendulum, its sleek body swayed from side to side in the air.

Propped up against huge silk pillows, a pale, sickly King Kilian lay in bed. His eyes were fixed upon the diamondback snake. His eleven-year-old granddaughter, Princess Bianca, sat beside him, her legs hanging over the edge of the King's bed. They both awaited the Wizard's performance. What magic would he conjure up this evening?

Bianca was puzzled by this man, Neechie. Was he a fake or did he really know magic? True, he did saw a maid in half last week without any pain or harm to her. But then again, if he really knew magic, why couldn't he make Grandfather well again or bring home Mom, she wondered. That's what I'd do if I knew magic, thought Bianca.

Her mother, Attena, left on a mission to another kingdom a year ago. But six months after she had departed, a messenger brought back word: Attena had died on her way home in a rock slide as she crossed the treacherous mountains separating the two kingdoms. Bianca, however, knew in her heart that somehow her mother had survived. She would return, someday.

Bianca studied her father, Prince Rip. His slight frame, slouched in an overstuffed chair, his thinning hair in disorder. He rustled through the evening newspaper, ignoring the Wizard.

Dad just hasn't been the same since Mom's accident, she thought. He seems more irritated with Neechie and his magic, or "parlor tricks" as he calls them. Her father said the Wizard had become a better entertainer than adviser.

Bianca glanced back at the Wizard and brushed aside a few strands of dark brown hair from her deep green eyes. Her thin eyebrows were knitted in concentration; he wouldn't fool her this time. "Roll up your sleeves," she suggested, pointing to his loose robe sleeves that draped down to his wrists.

"Don't worry, my dear Princess," the Wizard said sweetly. "I won't be sticking this snake up them."

"Dad, keep an eye on Neechie," Bianca called over to her father.

"No problem," he replied, now hidden behind the newspaper.

"Da-ad, please! I mean it," Bianca pleaded.

"OK, OK." Rip tossed the paper on the oak table beside him. Peering over his reading glasses, he asked, "All right Wiz, what are you going to do with that toy?"

"Toy, huh? Would you care to hold it?" The Wizard swung the hissing snake toward Rip's face.

"Thanks for the offer, but I'll pass," Rip said through clenched teeth.

"What are you going to do with the snake?" Bianca asked the Wizard, drawing his attention away from her father.

"Should I change it into bird?" he suggested, as his captive slowly twisted in the air.

"Change it into a canary, so it can join the others outside," Bianca said. Through the King's open window came a warm evening breeze laced with the birds' light, cheery songs. It was summertime and thousands of canaries nested in the cherry trees, lining the town plaza outside the palace.

The Wizard stroked his long, gray beard as if he were making an important, thoughtful decision. He relished making even the most minor decisions seem important.

He mumbled, "Perhaps." And then, pointing to an empty fruit basket resting on the King's bed, he said, "Bianca, please place that basket on the table next to your father."

She did as requested and then returned to her grandfather's side. King Kilian weakly patted his granddaughter's back.

The Wizard eased the snake into the basket. "Rip, after I release the snake, would you cover the top of the basket with your newspaper?" He grinned, baring yellow, worn teeth.

Rip sighed and nodded reluctantly.

"And do be careful. We wouldn't want any nasty bites," the Wizard added, releasing his hold on the snake.

Rip delicately covered the basket to avoid disturbing the viper.

The Wizard clasped the container with both hands so the newspaper could not slide off, and raised it above his head. He twirled three times; his silky, white robes floated around and about him as he chanted, "Trathus-Raza, Trathus-Raza, Trathus-Raza."

At the end of the third turn, he tore away the newspaper. A nerve-tingling shriek sliced through the room as a great black raven flew from the basket and out the window.

Startled, Bianca fell back but quickly righted herself and said, matter-of-factly, "A canary would have been better."

"The canary's song is certainly sweeter than the raven's caw, but canaries are weak and ravens are survivors," said the Wizard. "Those things that are weak, my dear Princess, are replaced by those that are stronger – those that will rule the future."

The Wizard then bowed and revealed an empty basket to his audience.

Chapter 2

Prince Rip's Future

The King was not amused by the Wizard's tricks this evening. He shook his head weakly and frowned. After a fitful breath, King Kilian spoke, "Rip, I've been thinking about something for awhile."

Rip rose and drew near his father. The Wizard trailed behind him, practically stepping on the Prince's heels. "Can I do anything?" Rip asked, laying his hand on the King's shoulder.

The Wizard pressed closely behind Rip.

Trembling, the sick King said, "Son, I've decided to abdicate and crown you the King of Tiara ... tomorrow."

"Tomorrow! That leaves little time to prepare," said the Wizard, teetering back on his heels.

Prepare for what? Bianca asked herself as she stared at the aged Wizard. She had resented him from the first day he arrived in their Kingdom a year ago.

He did bring the invitation from the Kingdom of Zurbia requesting Attena's help, which caused her to leave. And when her grandfather appointed him as the Wizard, right after her mother had left, it felt like an unwelcome stranger had moved into Bianca's home. While others addressed Neechie as the Wizard, she did not.

Nevertheless, like everyone else, Bianca was awed by his magic and his knowledge of the outside world. He said he had seen the future in Zurbia and that he could help Tiara. But she was never sure how. There was something about him, something about his manner and especially his wicked little jokes that unsettled her.

The King briefly fingered the Ruby Ring that hung from his gold neck chain. He softly said to himself, "My fingers have been too swollen this past year to wear it. And my illness has left me so weak that I can hardly stay awake, let alone listen to what others are thinking."

Bianca stared down at the ring and its mysterious ruby. As slowly as clouds drifting across the sky, the stone's color shifted from blood red to magenta.

Grandfather had said that whoever wore the Ruby Ring could read people's minds. Could he be listening to our thoughts now? wondered Bianca. Certainly if he could, he'd know if Neechie was evil.

"Are you sure you want to do this?" asked Rip.

"Yes, you must take the Ruby Ring as the next ruler of Tiara," the King instructed his son.

"Don't fear, Rip, under my guidance you can modernize Tiara," the Wizard said smoothly as he draped his arms across Rip and Bianca's shoulders.

"How would you modernize Tiara?" asked Bianca, squirming from his embrace.

"By giving up our isolation and joining the modern world. Let us learn from Zurbia, even with its imperfections, its wealth far outstrips Tiara's."

If he liked it so much, why didn't he stay there? He always thinks he knows more than the rest of us, she thought.

"Tiara needs to change, but not into another Zurbia," Rip said forcefully.

"I'll be calling a town council," Rip said, flashing a sly smile.

"What do you mean?" the Wizard asked, eyes narrowing.

"The people of Tiara need to be responsible for ruling themselves," Rip explained. "We've become too dependent on a king making the decisions. If we ever had a bad ruler, Tiara's very existence could be threatened."

"We should have discussed this first," the Wizard said abruptly. "A town council will lead to confusion - so many petty concerns, worthless opinions ...."

Rip cut him off with a wave of the hand. "Wizard, listen to what others have to say."

The Wizard shook his head. "You don't need to count noses. You'll be the king and I'll be your adviser. Why listen to others? They have no idea what the future holds. Your little kingdom can't remain cut off from reality forever, hopelessly trying to hold back progress."

The Wizard pointed a long pasty-white finger towards the window. "Look at that huge forest. It's going to waste, slowly rotting, becoming worthless. It's not there just for us to look at; it's there to be used. We could make Tiara richer than Zurbia. You don't have to remain a primitive, backward place where ...."

Again Rip cut him off. "Where we use bikes and horses instead of cars."

"That is precisely the problem!" the Wizard retorted, gripping Rip's arm. "It's time to give up these simple ways."

"Well, we differ on what Tiara's future should be," Rip said calmly. He pushed aside the Wizard's hand and turned to King Kilian. "As you wish, the coronation will take place tomorrow afternoon in the palace courtyard."

The Wizard leaned forward and spoke directly to the King. "I've served you well this past year. Please instruct your kind, but foolish son to heed my advice."

The King's eyelids drooped as he whispered, "I'm too weak and sick. Tiara is in Rip's hands." His eyes closed; the matter was settled.

Rip took Bianca's hand and they headed for the door.

But the Wizard raced ahead of them and barred their exit. He angrily jabbed his long finger into Rip's chest. "Your simple-minded solutions will rob us of a glorious and rich future."

"Perhaps the burden of being Tiara's Wizard should be lifted from your shoulders," Rip said, arching an eyebrow.

The Wizard slowly withdrew his finger, clenching his hand into a fist. "I thought you could learn from me. But I was wrong."

Then in an icy voice that chilled Bianca to the bone, he added, "Your future is doomed." He whipped around, his white robes swirling behind him, and stomped away.

CHAPTER 3

The Wizard's Plans

Bianca followed her father down the hallway. Upon reaching his den, Rip marched straight to his desk and began shuffling papers. Bianca, feeling ignored, slumped onto a cushion near a window. Rip was attracted to paper like a bee to a flower. If he wasn't hiding behind a newspaper, he was stacking sheets of paper into piles.

"You should go outside more often," Bianca suggested. Rip hunched over his desk and didn't reply. He didn't look as tan or as fit as he had last summer. More worry lines now creased his forehead. Bianca felt that he sorely missed her mother, but he didn't speak often of his feelings.

Seeing that he was deep in thought, Bianca gazed out the window. She looked over the town's yellow tile rooftops and beyond the great blue wall which encircled the town. The slow-moving, brownish River Po cut through the middle of Tiara's valley of small farms and pastures. High up on the other side of the valley began the Tygan Forest. It stretched on until it reached the white-capped Tygan Mountains. The Kingdom of Zurbia was beyond those jagged peaks.

"She left on a sunny day like this," Bianca said softly, thinking of her mother.

Rip remained silent. The rustling of his papers grew louder.

Bianca had always been proud of Attena's ability to solve problems. And so she was not too surprised when her mother received an invitation last summer to travel to the distant Kingdom of Zurbia.

Attena had promised to return before the first snows fell. But summer had faded and autumn had come without word from her. Just as Rip was preparing to journey out in search of her, word arrived of Attena's death.

"I wish she were here with us," Bianca said, a little louder.

The rustling stopped. Rip swiveled around in his chair and looked at Bianca. "Yes, I do, too," he said. Her words had brushed aside the wall of papers to reveal her father's large sad eyes.

Bianca left the window and joined him. Although no longer a small child, she still enjoyed sitting in her father's lap. "So, when do you think she'll be coming back?" she asked.

Rip ran his fingers up Bianca's high forehead and through her long hair. He was silent for a time, and then said, "You have to brush your hair. It's too tangled."

"Da-ad!" Bianca pushed her father's hand away. "Answer my question."

"Bianca," Rip said slipping his finger under her chin, "no matter how hard you wish, no matter how much you believe in magic, it won't change the fact that your mother is not coming back. You must grow up and be responsible. You will have to live your life - without magic.

"You make growing up sound so boring," Bianca said, jerking her head away.

"It's not boring. You get to create your future: to make our kingdom a better place to live for yourself and others."

"Just like Neechie wants to." Bianca's mockery was clearly evident.

"Hmm, the Wizard does get carried away with himself," Rip said.

"I just think that he can't be trusted. Why did Grandfather make him Tiara's Wizard, anyway?" she asked.

"Actually, it was my idea," Rip replied sheepishly. "I thought he could be helpful while your mother was gone. And I guess I was just looking for an easy solution to our problems. His technical knowledge helped our factories make more bricks than ever before. And as you know, we need more all the time to rebuild after the Vandal attacks."

Just the mention of the Vandals brought a shiver to Bianca. They were the scourge of the Earth. During the summer they would come through the mountain pass, raid their valley, and destroy both buildings and crops. Only a strong wall kept them from entering the town. Even the Wizard told of the chaos they had caused in Zurbia.

Rip went on, "And his parlor tricks did entertain the King. I didn't think making Neechie our Wizard was a big thing. But it seems to have gone to his head. His tricks have increasingly taken a dark turn," said Rip, frowning.

"Do you think he really knows magic?" Bianca asked her father for the hundredth time.

"Bianca, you find magic in fairy tales, not in the real world."

"Well he's convinced a lot of people he knows magic," Bianca persisted.

"Just other eleven-year-olds."

"Dad! Could he take control of Tiara?"

"He's just a harmless old man. Anyhow, as long as King Kilian or I have the Ruby Ring, nothing like that can happen," Rip replied with a wink.

Is he joking? Bianca wondered. Dad doesn't believe in magic. "Can King Kilian really hear someone's thoughts with the Ruby Ring?" she asked.

"To tell you the truth, I don't know," Rip admitted. "Father always said he'd tell me about the Ruby Ring, but he became ill and we never talked about it."

"But tomorrow you'll discover its powers," Bianca said.

"I suppose so," Rip said.

"Then you'll know what the Wizard is planning."

"Oh, I already know his plans." Rip sighed and took off his reading glasses. "He wants to mow down the forest."

"What for?" Bianca cried, jumping up. For Bianca, the forest was a like a great, comfortable blanket laid down between Tiara's valley and the distant Tygan Mountains. The Earth would seem bare without it. And, although she had never traveled deep into the forest, she did love playing in the groves near the valley, swinging from gnarly oak branches and scaling the ladder-like pines.

"He wants to build a road over the mountains to Zurbia. They would buy our logs, we'd make lots of money, and we could all buy cars," Rip said dryly.

"What would we do with cars?" She had seen pictures of them in books – they looked much bigger than bicycles. How could they drive down the town's narrow streets? And out in the valley, riding on a horse, under the sun with the wind blowing through her hair, seemed more fun than riding inside a big can.

"We could race them around the plaza, I suppose. But don't worry, your grandfather's ban on cars will remain. Anyhow, they can't make it over the mountains from Zurbia."

"Could Neechie change that?"

"No. It's impossible to build a road over the Tygans. The pass is too narrow for anything other than a horse or the Vandals' motorcycles."

His remarks eased her worries about Tiara's future. But as for her own...?

"Do you think Grandfather will...die?" she asked.

Rip raked his fingers through his thinning hair. He wearily replied, "Yes, I'm afraid so. He doesn't have much time left."

Bianca fell silent. With her mother gone and her grandfather dying, only her father was left of her family.

Anxiously, she asked, "You won't let anything happen to you, will you?"

"I'm not planning on it," Rip said, casually. "But just in case, I've let it be known to those in the palace that should I die my will would create a town council. And only a few loyal friends know where the will is hidden."

"I hate to think of things like that," Bianca said.

"I do too, but it insures my safety for awhile. We know certain people don't want to see one created, don't we?" Rip said.

"I guess everything should be OK," Bianca said. But still, she had this feeling... Something evil was brewing.

CHAPTER 4

The Coronation

The palace's four spires towered over the town. Their red bricks contrasted sharply with the yellow bricks of the other buildings and the blue bricks of the town wall. Tiara's palace was more than just a home for the royal family and a dozen of their loyal friends. It was Tiara's community center, hosting many social events. And the coronation was to be the biggest ever.

People throughout the kingdom streamed into the palace. There were farmers from the valley, and store owners and factory workers from inside the town. With much laughing and talking, guests strolled around the palace courtyard or sat at small tables eating the sweet corn and fresh fruit grown in the valley.

Bright red columns shaped like huge ears of corn lined the courtyard. Bianca stood next to one, talking to her friend Jewel, who lived in an orderly world of proper place-settings and rules. While Bianca might hand in her schoolwork a week late, Jewel was always a day early. But they were close friends, as they had both grown up in the palace, playing, studying and most importantly, trading secrets.

Although usually found in jeans and sweat-shirts, for the coronation they wore short-sleeved, white summer dresses. Royal purple headbands, worn only by palace residents, pulled their hair back.

Jewel's wavy red hair bobbed just above her shoulders as she munched on an apple. Despite appearing to eat all the time, she seemed as thin as a broom handle.

Bianca glanced occasionally from side to side while talking. She excitedly told Jewel about the previous evening and her dad's plan to call a town council after being crowned King.

"That makes sense," said Jewel.

"Neechie didn't think so," Bianca replied.

"He didn't?" said Jewel, surprised. While giving this some thought, she neatly folded a napkin around her apple core.

"He was actually furious," Bianca went on.

"But it's only fair to give everybody a chance to make rules," Jewel said. She shuffled the wrapped apple core between her hands, its proper resting place uncertain.

"Everybody can't make the rules," a sharp voice cracked from behind them.

Bianca and Jewel swung around to see the Wizard's teenage assistant, Bug. With his slicked-back dark hair and large bulging eyes, the nickname seemed fitting. Bianca had taken a dislike to him from the day he arrived in Tiara with the Wizard.

"A strong leader should make the rules. Someone who has traveled beyond this valley. Someone who has lived in Zurbia," Bug said, twirling a toothpick between his front teeth.

"You mean Neechie? Almost no one else has been there," said Bianca.

"You said it, Princess," Bug said smugly.

Bianca fumed at his goading. If only he were a bug, he'd be a smudge under her shoe.

"What's so great about Zurbia anyhow?" asked Jewel, scratching her freckled nose.

"It's exciting and it's fun. It's far bigger than Tiara, with dozens of buildings many times taller than this palace. They have cars and motorcycles. You can get anything you want. If you have money, of course."

"Neechie isn't going to make Tiara like Zurbia," Bianca said pointedly.

"Don't be so sure, Princess," Bug sneered and swaggered away.

Bianca watched him disappear into the crowd and a chill went through her. What is he up to? she wondered. Before she had much time to think about it, a young blond man tapped her on the shoulder.

"Prince Rip wants to see you," he said. Bianca hugged Jewel

good-bye and weaved her way through the crowded courtyard toward her father's table, just below the dais.

On her way there, she noticed the Wizard standing within the shadow of a column, handing Bug a glass. The Wizard's assistant walked over to Rip's table, and handed the glass to the Prince.

Rip stopped a lively discussion with his friends to take a drink. When he saw Bianca, he motioned for her to come and give him a hug.

"What are you drinking?" she asked, breaking his embrace. She suspiciously eyed his half empty-glass.

"Just some milk," said Rip.

"Let me see it." Bianca took the glass and sniffed it.

"Hey, it's not spoiled," Bug said defensively, standing near Rip.

Bianca ignored Bug and took a sip.

"Is it OK to drink?" asked Rip, laughing light-heartedly.

Bianca shrugged her shoulders. "It tastes just like milk. Yuk, I hate that stuff."

Rip chuckled, took the glass and gulped the rest down.

After setting it back on the table, a young woman attendant notified Rip that the coronation was about to begin. Rip took his daughter's hand and they started up the steps to the dais. Suddenly, Rip stumbled. Bianca caught his arm and steadied him. "Dad, are you OK?"

"Yes, but I've just become a bit dizzy." He rested his hand on her shoulder and squeezed it slightly.

It was a brief ceremony. King Kilian, Prince Rip, Bianca, the Wizard, and a few palace residents and townspeople stood on the dais. Below them, the talking and laughing had given way to a hush as the packed courtyard reverently observed the ceremony.

King Kilian appeared unsteady on his feet, as if the weight of his oversized purple cloak would buckle his legs at any moment.

He spoke in a low, raspy voice. "I crown Prince Rip the next King of Tiara. Work with him to keep our small kingdom in harmony with nature. Our simple ways have kept our valley's air and water pure, as well as our hearts. Do not abandon these real riches for promises of paper wealth."

Though everyone in the courtyard was respectfully attentive, Bianca wondered if they could hear his soft-spoken words.

With pale, shaking hands, the King placed his crown on his son's head. Rip yawned and rubbed his eyes.

King Kilian, a tired and painful expression on his face, removed the thin gold chain from which the Ruby Ring dangled. He slipped the ring off and handed it to his son.

Rip slid the Ruby Ring onto his finger. Not a minute had passed before his expression dramatically changed. He glared at the Wizard. Bianca watched her father and wondered what had angered him? Could he be reading Neechie's mind?

But the fire in Rip's eyes quickly dimmed. He blinked repeatedly and swayed on his feet. Easing himself into one of the large cushioned chairs on the dais, he motioned Bianca over to him.

He reached out, grabbed her sleeve and drew her near to him. With eyelids nearly closed, he whispered, "Bianca, we've been tricked. You must get to Zurbia. Attena ..." his voice trailed off.

His words exploded in her mind: "...Must get to Zurbia, Attena." So her mother was still there?

With a little start, Rip's eyes opened briefly. Struggling to be heard, he added, "Watch out for the Wizard!"

The Wizard? Her lips parted but no words came out. What was happening? Was she under a spell?

The courtyard swirled around her, sounds became faint and images blurred. Silently, slowly, she felt herself falling, falling into darkness.

CHAPTER 5

The New Ruler for Tiara

Bianca gradually became conscious of the Pax Flowers' sweet aroma. King Kilian had given them to her before he became ill. They now bloomed year round in her window's flower box.

Far below her window, the canaries sang. Feeling groggy, she sat up in bed and shook her head to wake herself. The last thing she remembered clearly was her conversation with Jewel. Everything after that was blurred.

Bianca slowly pulled on her jeans and slipped into a T-shirt. She scooped up a brush from her dresser and lazily brushed her hair. Don't want Dad finding any knots, she thought, and strolled down the stairway from her bedroom.

On the stairwell leading up to Rip's room, a dozen maids and palace residents stood whispering among themselves. One of the maids saw Bianca approaching and hushed the others to silence.

Bianca stopped brushing. "Good morning," she said. Their sad expressions disturbed her. Why were they here?

Silently they parted, clearing the way to Rip's room. She pressed against the door and it slowly swung open. Inside, her father lay on his bed. The Wizard was taking his pulse.

The bedroom windows were closed. The still, heavy air made her even drowsier. She felt as if she were floating into a bad dream. Her arms went limp. The hairbrush fell from her hand, hitting the hardwood floor with a sharp crack.

The Wizard looked up, his lifeless pale eyes locked onto hers.

"Your father's asleep," he said, without emotion.

"Is he sick?" Bianca asked, worried.

"It seems so. He can't be woken," the Wizard said coldly. "A strange bug may have bitten him, causing a sleeping sickness. He may sleep for a long time. Perhaps..." the Wizard stroked his thin gray beard, "a very long time."

The bad dream had become real. Her insides felt as if they had collapsed, her eyes filled with tears. Why did this happen?

"We were concerned about you as well," said a maid standing behind her.

"Why?" Bianca's voice was barely a whisper.

"You fainted at the coronation. And, you slept all day."

"Fainted...? Slept all day...?" She asked weakly, trying to gather her thoughts.

"Maybe you had the same thing," said Bug, from the far side of the room.

Bianca tried focusing on him. An image of Bug from last night teased her. After leaving Jewel, hadn't she seen Neechie hand him something?

The Wizard moved away from Rip's bed. He raised his arms and said, "Let's leave King Rip alone for awhile. It's not good to have so many people around him. Germs you know, that sort of thing."

He then spoke to Bianca. "I've called for a town gathering in the plaza to tell everyone what has happened."

Silently, Bianca started walking over to her dad. Before reaching the bed, the Wizard wrapped his arm around her and spun her toward the door. Sternly, he said, "You can visit your father after my public announcement."

She wanted to break away but her legs and arms still felt heavy with sleep.

Within an hour the Wizard was addressing the townspeople from the palace's balcony. Bianca stood beside him. Sounding like a doctor, he told those gathered in the plaza below of Rip's illness.

Then, clearing his throat, he announced, "I'm afraid I must also tell you that our dear King Kilian passed away last night."

A sharp pain ripped through Bianca. Neechie is mean-hearted and cruel, thought Bianca. Why didn't he tell me? Tears poured down her cheeks. She shuddered at the thought of being alone now, without a family.

Mother said to be strong, but it's hard when there's no one to hold onto for comfort, she thought. She looked down upon a sea of faces staring up at her. Can't let them see me crying, she reasoned, they'll think I'm just some poor, weak girl. With a determined swipe of a sleeve she wiped her tears away.

Booming with authority, the Wizard declared, "Until King Rip wakes from his sleep, Princess Bianca is the new ruler of Tiara."

Bianca thought, I can't rule Tiara. I'm only a kid. And I don't want to sit at a desk all day moving pieces of paper around. I want to go outside and play.

All those people staring at me, wanting me to be like my parents, she thought. But I don't know how. She stepped back from the balcony railing and flattened herself against the wall behind the Wizard.

When the crowd's chatter had died down, the Wizard continued, "Since Bianca is a minor, according to the law, I am her guardian."

I haven't heard of this law, she thought. Neechie must have tricked Grandfather into making it without Dad's knowledge.

Yet, Bianca felt strangely relieved that she would not be responsible for leading Tiara. On the other hand, it made her sick to think of the Wizard ruling Tiara. He'll ruin everything, she fumed. He'd probably even cut down the cherry trees in our plaza.

Anger jolted her memory. Suddenly she recalled her father's last words, "Watch out for the Wizard." Her emotions flared, her heart pounded wildly against her chest. The battle was on, Neechie must not gain control of Tiara.

Then she remembered the Ruby Ring. If it does have magic, he mustn't have it.

The Wizard's back was toward her as he looked down onto the plaza. She had to act now. Without being noticed, she edged off the balcony exit and with new-found energy ran to Rip's room.

Since the Wizard had insisted that everyone in the palace attend his speech, the halls were empty. Luckily he hadn't posted guards outside Rip's bedroom.

She pushed open the door. Her father was alone, snoring in bed. The old wood-plank floor creaked slightly as she crept to Rip's side.

Bianca kissed his forehead and glanced down. He still wore the Ruby Ring. Ha! Neechie was so sure of his power, he left the Ring unguarded. She quickly twisted it off her father's finger.

But she dared not wear it, fearing the Wizard would somehow take it away. Instead she would hide it. But where?

Bianca looked down from Rip's bedroom window. The Wizard was still speaking from the main balcony.

She opened the window just a crack to better hear him. "The people of Tiara must learn to work faster. The faster you work, the more you'll earn and the more things you can own," he was telling the crowd.

Then the Wizard thrust his arm out from his side, reaching for Bianca. When he realized she was gone, he seemed bewildered. Turning back to the crowd, he abruptly ended his speech and dismissed his audience.

He may come for the Ruby Ring, Bianca thought. She peeked out the bedroom door. The stairwell leading up to Rip's room was still empty and silent. She shoved the Ruby Ring into her pocket and raced down the stairs.

CHAPTER 6

A Time to Take Control

Rip's room, like Bianca's, occupied one of the palace's four spires. Each of the spires connected to the palace's main hallway by a long stairway.

Bianca had turned a corner in the hallway when she saw the Wizard. He was at the far end of the corridor, running toward her, his cape flapping off his back like a bed sheet in the wind.

She ducked behind a large urn, hoping he hadn't seen her. His puffing got louder as he ran toward her hiding spot. She squeezed herself between the urn and the hallway wall.

His footsteps stopped a few feet away, but his panting continued. Had he stopped to catch his breath? Slowly the panting became fainter. Was he walking away or breathing easier?

Unable to hold back her curiosity, Bianca peered over the urn. He was walking away, toward Rip's spire. Quietly, she slipped out of her hiding place and ran down the hall.

Taking two steps at a time, she bounded up the stairs of her spire. Her heart was racing when she reached her door. She opened it gently, half expecting to find Bug or a palace guard waiting for her, but the room was empty.

Neechie's going to be upset when he finds the Ruby Ring gone, she thought. And I'm sure he'll think I took it.

She pulled the Ruby Ring from her pocket. Have to find a place to hide you, she thought, sliding open a dresser drawer. She emptied a small leather pouch of two quartz crystals and dropped the Ruby Ring into it.

But her room was not a safe hiding place. She opened her door again and spotted a loose brick in one of the stairs. Moving quickly, she slid the brick out, shoved the pouch under it and then returned the brick to its original position.

She breathed a sigh of relief – the ring was safely hidden.

Retreating to her room, she flung herself face down across her bed. She was overwhelmed by the whirl of happenings: her grandfather's death, her father's sleeping sickness, and now Neechie's guardianship.

Her world had been turned inside out. There must be a way to straighten it all out, she told herself. Her father's words drifted through her mind, like a voice in a dream: "Get to Zurbia." That's it! she thought. Dad must have believed that Mom is still there. Why else would he have told me to go Zurbia.

But to reach Zurbia meant traveling through the Tygan Forest and over the Tygan Mountains. Up to now she had only visited the forest in the area immediately around their valley.

It was too dangerous to make the journey alone. She needed a companion to help fend off the Vandals that roamed the forest. Her friend Lara came to mind. She was Tiara's best sentry and had fought Vandals. I must convince her to go with me, Bianca thought.

Just then the dinner bell rang. She didn't look forward to the meal. All of the palace residents would be present.

They'll expect me to talk and act like an adult, she thought. They'll want to know what I'm going to do for our Kingdom. And then again, what will I say if Neechie mentions the Ruby Ring? Doubts whirled around inside her mind, tugging her down into despair.

The bell rang a second time, now sounding like an alarm clock going off, shaking her out of her stupor. It was time to get up and take control of her life.

Twenty of the palace residents sat waiting for Bianca at the dinner table. When she entered, they rose and bowed slightly. Bianca smiled awkwardly.

The Wizard wore a big, friendly grin and said, "Please sit at the head of the table. That's where Rip would have sat. I'll sit right next to you. Bug will sit on your other side."

Bianca glared at him. Jewel, not Bug, had always sat next to her at dinner. "Bug, Jewel is sitting next to me, not you," she said.

Bug's eyes widened and then he glanced at the Wizard, who

nodded his approval. With a scowl and huffing with resentment, Bug shuffled to another seat.

Jewel practically skipped up to Bianca and took her rightful place.

After some time, it occurred to Bianca that this meal was different from past ones. Previously, people talked to one another over dinner. She usually didn't talk herself, feeling more comfortable listening. Now there was nothing to listen to, except the clanking of forks and spoons against the dinner plates.

They're feeling sad about Grandfather's death and Dad's illness, she thought. But even so, she felt it was something else.

Bianca glanced at the Wizard, who looked smugly contented. She nudged Jewel. Almost whispering she asked her, "Why isn't anyone talking?"

"Before you came down to dinner, the Wizard said that we should eat in silence from now on," Jewel replied.

"But why?"

"He said there had been too much talking and laughing. He says we should spend more time thinking about our work."

"That's stupid," Bianca said under her breath and then surveyed the faces around the table. She nudged Jewel again and whispered, "They're afraid of him, aren't they?"

Swallowing her food, Jewel looked at Bianca and said, "Yes, and I'm afraid, too."

A moment after Jewel spoke, the Wizard abruptly stood up. He raised his arms high over his head. His long white robes flowed down from his shoulders and arms. In a single wave of brilliant white, he clapped his hands. The sound echoed off the walls like thunder.

"I have an important announcement to make: the Ruby Ring is missing!" The Wizard's voice boomed through the dining hall.

For the first time during the meal, people began talking. Their murmuring became steadily louder and louder.

Bianca wondered if she should say anything. Before she could speak, Mr. Popolo, an old friend of her father's, rose to his feet. He had a large round tummy and thick arms. His eyes were large and his head was covered with curly dark hair. He was the largest person living in town.

"The Ruby Ring is Tiara's most valuable possession. We must find it before it gets lost," said Mr. Popolo.

Smirking, the Wizard snapped at him, "Mr. Popolo, it is lost!"

Suddenly, the large dining room window shattered, raining broken glass down upon everyone. A second later several beer bottles flew through the gaping hole in the window and crashed near the dining table.

"Vandals!" yelled Mr. Popolo, rushing to the shattered window. More beer bottles crashed through the other windows. "They're lobbing them over our wall, probably with one of their giant slingshots," he said. A bottle just missed his head as it smashed onto the table and splintered over it.

"Run for cover!" screamed Mrs. Popolo. Although not as big as Mr. Popolo, she was Tiara's second largest citizen. She overturned several chairs in her charge from the table. A man running behind her tumbled over one. He flung his hands out to break his fall. His palms slammed against the broken glass covering floor. A smeared line of bright red blood marked his painful slide.

Soon everyone in the room was rushing for the exit, as shards of glass flew through the air, nicking them.

Bianca grabbed Jewel's hand. "Let's get out of here," she yelled. They ran for the exit, but as Bianca left the room, she glanced back.

The Wizard stood alone at the table, his white robes soaked with beer. Angrily, he waved a bony finger at her, as if about to speak.

Fear prickled down Bianca's spine. Not waiting to listen, she turned and sped down the hallway with Jewel.

CHAPTER 7

Searching for a Traveling Companion

B ianca and Jewel retreated to Bianca's bedroom to watch the Vandals. About a dozen of them clustered outside Tiara's blue wall.

The Vandals were yelling and revving up their black motorcycles. The high-pitched whine of their engines echoed throughout the city.

"Their attacks seem to be getting worse," said Jewel, hands on her slender hips. "They just come riding into our valley and wreck everything," she said turning to Bianca. "Why do they behave that way?"

"Grandfather said they spent too much time inside watching TV at day care," said Bianca. "All they knew about were cartoons and game shows, but nothing about the natural world. I guess they see everything as just a game."

"Well, I didn't like their game tonight. Do you think they'll get over our wall?" Jewel fretted, her hands now clenched into fists at her sides.

"There's too few of them. I'm sure they'll get bored and ride back into the forest." Overall, Bianca was more annoyed than scared by the Vandals this time.

The Wizard was a bigger threat to her. "Jewel, it looks like things will now be different in Tiara."

"You're right. When it was announced that you would be the ruler, I felt great. But the Wizard is taking over. He said that from now on only people he approves can enter the palace."

"I hadn't heard that," Bianca cried. "Next thing you know, he'll stop us from leaving the palace." Bianca slammed her hand against the wall. "I have to get to Zurbia."

Jewel's mouth gaped.

Bianca slowly added, "I don't want to see father sleeping forever. And it's the only way to stop Neechie from controlling Tiara."

Jewel grew pale. Her freckles seemed to multiply against her too-white skin. "Bianca, think about it. Getting to Zurbia is almost impossible. Vandals are out there. And there's Wood Nymphs, too. They could change you into a mushroom or a tree stump or whatever."

"They only do that to people who harm the forest, like the Vandals," Bianca assured her friend and herself. "Anyhow I'm going to ask Lara to join me."

"She's our best sentry but still..." Jewel's voice trailed off in doubt.

"You can come too," Bianca offered. She knew that Jewel was strictly a town kid. But she had a very logical mind that lead her to be cautious. Certainly a little caution in traveling through the forest might help Bianca avoid some dangers.

Jewel seemed agitated. "I don't understand. Why go to Zurbia?"

"Dad told me to go and I think Mom may still be there," Bianca said.

Jewel paced the room. "Bianca, I don't think we could get to Zurbia. How would we survive in the forest? How would we even feed ourselves?" She flailed her arms in emphasis. "If your mom was alive, she would have come back by now. Please don't go. It's too dangerous."

"I know it's dangerous," Bianca said, reflecting on her friend's advice. "But ... I have to."

Jewel lowered her eyes. "I'm not as brave as you. I don't think my parents would let me go even if I wanted to." She looked up. "But, I'll talk to them and see what they say."

Bianca gave Jewel a hug. "I'm not braver than you. It's just that your parents are here and now both of mine are ... gone." Bianca thought sadly about her poor father, perhaps sleeping forever, never holding her again. "I'm going to see Lara," she said softly and left the room.

On the way out of the palace, Bianca walked through the den. Jewel's brother Laser sat at a table tinkering with some gadgets. His unruly red hair looked as if it had never met a brush. A Milky Way of freckles spread from ear to ear. And, it seemed to Bianca, that he never wore anything other than his father's oversized blue work shirts, usually rolled up to his elbows.

And, like his father, too, he loved gadgets. A belt of them always hung from his waist, just like the one his father, Normal, wore.

Normal was Tiara's recycling engineer, and he used his gadgets and skills to make sure that Tiara's factories recycled the Kingdom's waste efficiently. Garbage was composted into rich soil for farming; those things that could not be composted were compressed and molded into red, yellow and blue compact bricks. The palace and other buildings were built with smooth red and yellow bricks. Tiara's town wall was built from rough blue ones.

Laser ignored Bianca as she entered the room and walked over to his table. She began casually toying with some of the wires and glass tubes. "So, what are you making now?" she asked.

"I don't know for sure," Laser said, fussing with some wires attached to a gizmo with tubes sticking out of it. "Maybe a machine to make you invisible. Then I wouldn't have to look at you," he added, snickering. Although he was a year older than Bianca, she was convinced he could never act his age.

"Very funny," Bianca said, and rolled her eyes.

After a moment of thought, she asked, "Laser, have you ever traveled through the forest?" If he had, she could as well. She was as smart and brave as he was.

"Not often, just a few times with Pop near the valley. Things get pretty spooky the deeper you go into the forest. You never know when the Vandals might ride up on their cycles." Laser wasn't joking this time.

"But you know, when I see the Tygans, I think about travel-

ing to Zurbia. The Wizard says it's quite different and more exciting than here," Laser said, looking out the den's large bay window. His attention drifted away.

Bianca stood at the edge of the table, twirling some of the
tubes that lay in front of her. She liked Laser but she couldn't
travel with him. He'd always be laughing at the wrong times and
embarrassing her.

She left him to his thoughts and slipped silently away. In the
foyer she found two palace guards, standing at attention on
either side of the large front doors. This was something new.
There had never been guards before.

"Is there something wrong?" she asked one of them.

A handsome young man replied, "Princess Bianca, the
Wizard said that the palace residents would be safer if guards
were stationed at the entrance at all times."

"Safe from what?"

"From Vandal attacks, like the one tonight," the guard
replied.

"But they were just throwing beer bottles. Our sentries
would guard us from any real attacks."

"Perhaps, but the Wizard also wants to keep strangers from
entering the palace. And rules are rules."

"That's never happened before," protested Bianca.
"Anyhow, I'm the Princess here, I say we don't need them."

"True, you are the Princess, but the Wizard is your guardian
and he knows what is best. When you get older, you can take
more responsibility," said the other guard, who was a middle-
aged, beer-bellied fellow with a large mustache.

His attitude infuriated Bianca, as she considered punching
him. But it was useless to argue. They're used to having adults
give orders, she thought. They couldn't imagine someone her
age being right.

She reached for the door handle, but the fat, older guard
stopped her. "Princess Bianca, you must be careful walking
around Tiara at night. I'll have a palace guard walk with you."

"I won't need one. Tiara is always safe. And the Vandals must have left; it's quiet now," she insisted.

The older guard twirled his mustache and winked at the younger guard. Gruffly, he said, "If you insist on going out, we can't be responsible for your safety."

He's trying to keep me from leaving the palace, she thought. But it won't work, I've got to see Lara. "That's OK, I can take of myself," she tartly replied and swung open the door.

As she walked away, one of the guards called out for the Wizard. She dreaded him finding out about her walk. But then again, what could he do?

CHAPTER 8

A Stroll at Night

Bianca strolled across the town plaza and headed down one of the many narrow, twisting streets that led from it. The streets of Tiara formed a giant maze, which served to confound any invader breaching the town's wall. The townspeople, on the other hand, knew the layout of the streets by heart.

The maze also served a second purpose. It forced people to slow down. It did no good rushing from one place to another since it always took a long time to get somewhere. So the people of Tiara learned to stroll leisurely about their town, with little need to wear watches or look at clocks to see if they were late.

Bianca reached the open meadows, located just inside Tiara's wall, and saw giant silver bubbles dotting the landscape. These were the homes of Tiara's sentries, who patrolled the wall and defended the town.

Against a dark sea of green grass, the dwellings glistened like dew drops under the moonlight. Their thick glass domes served as one-way mirrors, allowing the sentries to look out of them without being seen.

Upon reaching Lara's dwelling, she heard a violin playing a melancholy tune. It was as clear and natural as the full moon that shone above in the night sky.

Lara's door was open. Like all bubble homes, its door slid open like a large eyelid, revealing everything inside. Lara was leaning back in her favorite straight-legged wooden chair. Her bare feet rested on a table while she played the violin. She wore black jeans and a white blouse. Her dark frizzy hair made her appear wild, but the music she played was as peaceful as a purring cat.

Bianca listened for a while outside. She thought about the coming journey. Lara's help was absolutely necessary – without her it would be impossible.

Finally, Lara put down her violin and spotted Bianca. "Have you been standing there very long?" she asked.

"Not too long. I like listening to your music. It makes me feel good."

"Thanks for the compliment. Come in and have some hot cocoa," Lara beckoned.

Bianca carefully made her way around the books that littered the floor and pulled up a chair while Lara heated a pan of milk. Although only fifteen, Lara acted much older. She was poised, physically strong, and well-read.

At the age of seven, she had lost her parents to the Vandals. They had set Lara's farmhouse on fire one night. Her mother had perished in the flames and her father was never seen again. Some said the Vandals had taken him prisoner and then killed him. But others whispered that he had actually joined them.

Lara had somehow managed to escape unharmed and was raised by Tiara's sentries. Although almost a half-foot shorter than the average six-foot sentry, her natural grace endowed her with unmatched speed and agility.

Lara handed Bianca a cup and said, "I cried when I heard about King Kilian's death. He always encouraged me to read. Half of these books are from him," she said, gesturing to several stacks next to her bed.

If she thought of her grandfather again, Bianca knew she would start crying. And that wouldn't do any good now, she needed to concentrate on a solution.

"With your dad stricken with sleeping sickness, it must be hard on you. But remember, you have many friends to help you."

Bianca looked up from her cup and sighed. "What about Neechie?"

"Oh," Lara said, standing up and stretching out her long arms. She walked over to the stove and refilled her cup. "Word travels fast. I've heard he's making all sorts of new rules."

"And he's supposed to be my guardian." Bianca swirled the cocoa in her cup. "I feel more like a prisoner than the ruler of Tiara."

"People are used to having the rules made by just one person at the top. They're not likely to challenge his authority," reasoned Lara.

Bianca sipped her hot cocoa and admired Lara's smooth, light brown skin. She is so perfect, thought Bianca. I bet she wouldn't hesitate to go to Zurbia. But would she come with me?

"Lara, I think Mom's still in Zurbia."

Lara smiled sadly. "Bianca, if your mother were alive she would have returned long ago."

"That's what everybody thinks, but the last thing Dad told me was to go to Zurbia. And then he mentioned Mom. She must still be alive."

Lara walked over to the bubble's opening, studied the moon overhead with her large brown eyes and said, "I've thought of going to Zurbia, too. Sometimes I think that Dad is alive on the other side of the Tygans. Maybe the Vandals didn't kill him."

"Then you know how I feel," Bianca said earnestly.

"Sure," said Lara. She looked at Bianca and heaved a sigh. "I wish I could find my Dad."

"So we both have a reason to go there," said Bianca. "Will you help me? I don't know who else to ask."

"It'll be difficult. Few have traveled to Zurbia," said Lara. Then slowly a smile broke across her face. "But we should give it a try."

CHAPTER 9

Being Stalked

Although relieved that Lara would be her traveling companion, there were still dangers ahead. All of Jewel's warnings came to mind.

If only she knew magic, the journey would be safer. But only Neechie knew magic. Then she thought of the Wood Nymphs. King Kilian had told her they practiced magic. Her parents said they didn't even exist, but Bianca knew better.

"Do you know the Wood Nymphs? Do you think they would help us get to Zurbia?" she asked Lara.

"Well, I know Mrs. Arbor and she knows them. I've never seen them myself."

"I remember Mrs. Arbor. Dad took me to her daycare once," said Bianca. "She has a large, old house just inside the forest, doesn't she?"

"Yes," answered Lara. "Some of the valley people leave their children at her home while they work in the fields."

"Let's visit her on our way to Zurbia," Bianca suggested.

"When should we leave?" Lara asked, sitting back down in her chair.

Soon, Bianca thought. Before I lose my nerve. "Tomorrow," she blurted.

"That's probably good. The longer you stay, the more the Wizard will try to keep you in the palace. If he keeps you away from the townspeople, he can tell them whatever he likes in your name," Lara said.

"I think you're right. I was just hassled by his guards when I left the palace," Bianca told her.

"Do you think your dad will be safe if you leave?" Lara asked softly.

"He'll be safe. Neechie knows Dad made a will creating a town council and he'll want to keep Dad alive so the will isn't read," said Bianca. "And he won't be able to find it either, because only a few people know where Dad hid it."

"I hope it's well hidden," Lara said with concern. "If the Wizard found it, he could change the wording to make himself the next ruler, rather than just being your guardian," said Lara.

"He'd have to be a mind reader to find out who knows where it's hidden," Bianca assured her.

"He could use the Ruby Ring to read their minds," countered Lara.

"He won't be able to, I hid it," Bianca said, feeling smug.

"Does he know that?"

"I think he suspects me," said Bianca.

"Then you're in danger," Lara warned her friend.

Bianca nodded and said, "Let's leave after breakfast."

"I'll go to the palace early in the morning and load our bikes with supplies. If we leave before noon, we should get to Mrs. Arbor's house before nightfall," said Lara.

"We'll need horses to get over the mountains," said Bianca.

"No problem," replied Lara. "We can get some from the valley the next day."

The adventure would begin tomorrow, Bianca thought excitedly. She couldn't imagine sleeping tonight. But the stars had been out a long time; she had to return to the palace. After agreeing to see Lara at breakfast, Bianca crossed the meadow and entered the maze of streets.

She moved like a breeze along the deserted tree-lined avenues. Though deep in thought about her impending journey, she became aware of a noise behind her other than the rustling leaves. Something seemed to be scuffing against the street surface.

The noise stopped when she looked around, but she could see nothing. She continued on, but this time walked faster, alert to any unusual sounds.

A gentle breeze stirred the trees. I wonder how much I imagine and how much is real, she mused. Just then the sound of heavy boots thumping against the pavement cut through the evening stillness. It <u>wasn't</u> her imagination.

Bianca whirled around and peered down the street. But she couldn't see very far before the street sharply angled off to the right. The trees' moon shadows cast a kaleidoscope of geometric patterns along the pavement.

Was she being followed? If so, by whom? Could Neechie have sent someone? She looked up around her. All the windows were closed and dark.

Just then a huge shadow emerged from around the corner. Her legs felt weak. Trying to sound as grown up as possible, she called out, "Who's there?"

"Princess Bianca, it's I, Mr. Popolo," said a husky voice.

"I can't see you very well. Please come closer," Bianca said nervously. But how near did she want this shadowy figure?

Into the full moon's light stepped the huge body of Mr. Popolo.

"I was a little scared," said a relieved Bianca. "I didn't know who it was. Why in the world are you walking around here at night?"

"The guards told the Wizard that you had taken a walk. He was worried about your safety and asked me to look for you."

Bianca doubted the Wizard's concern for her safety. "Well, I'm OK. I just visited Lara." Bianca's friend was well known to the palace residents because of her friendship with the King and Bianca.

"I'll walk you back to the palace," offered Mr. Popolo. Bianca consented, although she was a bit suspicious of his intentions since he had been sent by Neechie. At the palace, Bianca thanked Mr. Popolo for the escort and then headed up to her bedroom.

As she ascended the stairs to her room, she noticed her door was ajar. A dim light shone from within. She hesitated a moment, wondering who could be waiting for her in the middle of the night. Then she pushed the door open.

CHAPTER 10

Challenging the Wizard

Bianca peered inside her room; a single candle flickered, casting a soft glow. Wavering shadows played on the walls of the empty room. Or was it? Someone, or something, moved under her bed cover. Had Neechie left a little surprise for her - something a bit more dangerous than his raven?

Bianca scanned the room for a weapon. She settled on an empty vase. With one hand gripping the vase, ready to strike, she ripped the cover off her bed.

Jewel rubbed her eyes and yawned. "You're back. I fell asleep waiting for you."

Bianca sighed loudly, replaced the ugly vase and closed the bedroom door. "Am I glad to see you here. Neechie is making this place creepy," she said with a shudder.

"He came by earlier looking for you," said Jewel, eyes closing slowly. "I decided to stay in case you needed me."

"Thanks. But soon I won't have to worry about him. Tomorrow, Lara and I leave for Zurbia," Bianca declared.

"I'm glad for you," said Jewel, yawning and seemingly unaware of exactly what Bianca had said. A moment later, she was fast asleep.

Bianca changed into her nightgown, and slid under the covers. The long and exhausting day brought a deep, peaceful sleep.

Bianca awoke to the morning sunlight warming her face and the delightful sound of canaries chirping in the courtyard. She sat up in bed, feeling refreshed and clear-headed.

"Today I begin my adventure," Bianca said aloud to herself.

Jewel was already dressed and standing near the door. "I'll talk to my parents this morning about going to Zurbia."

"Make sure they don't tell anyone," cautioned Bianca.

"They won't," said Jewel.

"I want you to come along, but it will be dangerous. Perhaps..." Bianca hesitated.

"I can take care of myself," Jewel said, confidently adjusting her head band as she left the room.

Bianca leaped out of bed and stuffed her knapsack. The Ruby Ring came to mind: should she leave it hidden in the palace or take it?

Deciding to look at the ruby one more time, she carefully removed it from its hiding place and brought it into her room. She opened the leather pouch and held the ring in the palm of her hand near the open window.

The morning sunlight played off the Ruby's shifting red colors. It's almost as if it were alive, thought Bianca, sliding the tips of her fingers across its smooth round surface.

"Here's my chance - she's alone. Either I find out where the Ruby is or she'll have a little accident."

Bianca's heart skipped a beat. The words were like whispers in her head. But they were as clear as if they had been spoken aloud.

She quickly made a fist around the Ruby Ring. Turning to face her visitor, she casually stuck both hands into the pockets of her jeans.

The Wizard's cold pale eyes starred down on her. He stroked his beard, eyeing her up and down.

Bianca gathered her nerve and said, "Tell me. When will Dad wake up?" The Ruby Ring grew warmer in her fist.

The Wizard stopped stroking his beard and stiffened his back. He didn't like her assertive tone. *"I wonder if she suspects that Rip drank a sleeping potion?"*

Bianca's eyes grew wide as she heard the Wizard's thoughts.

"Why does she look surprised? I haven't said anything. Unless... she's reading my mind. She must have the Ruby Ring on her!"

Bianca then heard the word *"ohm"* repeated over and over in her mind. She guessed he was chanting so she couldn't read his thoughts.

He stepped closer to Bianca, blocking her way to the door. Slowly she backed toward the open window.

"Hey Bianca, you're going to be late for breakfast," Laser yelled as he ran into the room.

The Wizard turned and laughed uncomfortably. "Yes, hurry along," he said looking back at Bianca.

Then slowly and deliberately he added, "I'll see you afterward – dear." The last word was drawn out like a sword, pointing directly at Bianca.

Before Bianca could reply, Laser grabbed her wrist and led her to the door. She dropped the Ruby Ring into her pocket, and, looking over her shoulder she carelessly teased the Wizard, "See me while you can." Then she and Laser ran down the stairs.

As they were about to enter the dining room, Bianca told Laser she wanted to visit her dad for a few minutes. He shrugged and said "I'm not going to save you any food."

"I'll be right back," she assured him.

Bianca opened the door to her father's bedroom to find him snoring. She kissed his forehead. "I'm going to find Mom and bring her back. I promise, Dad."

She pulled the Ruby Ring and pouch out of her pockets. No use leaving you here, she thought. I hope you can help me get to Zurbia. She plucked a leather cord from Rip's shelf and attached the pouch to it, then dropped the Ruby Ring into it.

Slipping the cord around her neck, she thought, I could use some magic on this trip.

CHAPTER 11

The Journey Begins

B ianca met Jewel in the hallway outside the dining room. "What did your parents say about going to Zurbia?"

"They said it was too dangerous for me, or you, to go," Jewel answered sadly. Then smiling, she added, "But, I dreamed last night that I did go. Perhaps it'll happen."

Bianca hugged her friend. "I feel that way, too," she said as they entered the dining room.

For the first time ever, palace guards stood at attention alongside the room's walls. *Neechie is tightening his grip on the palace,* she thought. *Perhaps we should have skipped breakfast and left at daybreak.*

As she sat down, the Wizard loudly cleared his throat. He turned and asked Bianca if she wished to address the palace residents.

Bianca stared back at him. She would not be intimidated. Lightly, her fingers touched the pouch underneath her sweatshirt, but she couldn't hear his thoughts. The Ruby Ring wasn't working.

"Bianca, don't daydream. We're waiting for you to speak. This is your first full day as our new ruler," the Wizard said, stiffly.

A table of familiar faces studied her. They were her friends, but they were too intimidated to challenge the Wizard's authority. She wanted to tell them not to worry, that she would bring Attena back. But she dare not mention it, fearing that the Wizard would stop her from leaving or have her ambushed on the way.

Neechie must believe that I accept his authority, she thought. A knot tightened in her stomach as she stood to speak. She had to say the right things, or she might not be able to get out of the palace.

Her words rolled out slowly. "Thank you for your sympathy. King Kilian and my father would have liked to see all of you help keep Tiara ..." She searched for the right thing to say. The back of her head felt the intensity of the Wizard's glare. He was weighing her every word. "... safe from the Vandals, and continue as a good place to live." They were safe, bland words.

She glanced up at the Wizard. He was reserving judgment. She needed to win him over. "I'm sure with the Wizard's guidance this can be accomplished." His thin lips curled up. He was pleased.

No need to say anymore, she thought, sitting down. The rest of the meal was eaten under the new regime of silence. Never had a meal lasted so long.

After breakfast, she thanked the Wizard for his help and excused herself from the room. Her casual stride masked her excitement and her pounding heart.

Lara was waiting for her in the plaza with both of their bikes. But she wasn't alone. Mr. Popolo was standing next to her with his bike. What was he doing here?

"Jewel's mother told me of your plans," Mr. Popolo said as she approached him. Bianca's face went white. How could she do that? This could ruin their plans.

"She thought I could help protect you on your trip. And, she knew that I was one of your father's closest friends."

Bianca looked at Lara. She shrugged, indicating it was Bianca's decision as to whether Mr. Popolo should join them.

"Did you tell anyone about this journey?" Bianca curtly asked him. "You didn't tell the Wizard, did you?"

He squirmed slightly under the sharp questioning and avoided her eyes. "I only told him we were going for a bike ride. I had to tell him something. He saw me coming here."

Bianca looked around the plaza. She was furious and she was scared. A few guards were standing in front the palace's main entrance and couple more were walking across the plaza toward them. Although Neechie was no where to be seen, she sensed his presence.

"Let's get going," suggested Lara, impatiently. "I don't want the Wizard showing up and asking questions. He might send his guards with us."

Bianca agreed. There was no time to waste being angry or upset. They bicycled through Tiara's maze of streets and across the open meadow to the blue wall. Just in case of any last-

minute problems, Lara had made sure some trusted sentries would let her through the main gate. The doors swung open and out they rode, coasting down the slope.

Mr. Popolo took the lead, leaving Lara and Bianca a ways behind him.

"He looks like a pear balanced on the edge of coin, doesn't he?" observed Lara.

"It's a wonder he can keep his balance," Bianca replied.

"You were upset about his coming along," said Lara.

"Yes. I know he's an old friend of Dad's. But still, Neechie may have given him some kind of potion. It could have changed him in some way. I found out he slipped one to Dad. And now he can't be awakened."

Lara kept pedaling, looking straight ahead. "Are you sure the Wizard did that?"

"Yes. He mixed a sleeping potion into Dad's glass of milk at the coronation."

"When did you find out?"

"I wasn't sure until this morning when I was holding the Ruby Ring. Neechie came into my room and I heard his thoughts.

"I guess I must have swallowed some of the potion too, when I took a sip from Dad's glass, because I fainted and slept most of the next day," Bianca explained.

"Do you still have the Ruby?" Lara asked.

"Yes. And Neechie knows I have it."

Lara frowned. "That means he'll be coming after us."

Part Two: JOURNEY TO ZURBIA

CHAPTER 12

Into the Tygan Forest

Bianca and Lara easily caught up with Mr. Popolo going up the other side of the valley. Sweat oozed from his forehead and trickled down his fat, flushed cheeks. "This is a good way to lose weight," he said panting.

"I think we should stop at the top of this hill for a brief rest," Bianca suggested.

"Good idea! – We can look over – the valley one last time – before entering the forest," he said, huffing and puffing.

Lara proposed a picnic and Mr. Popolo vigorously nodded in agreement.

While picnicking, they took in Tiara's valley of corn fields and large cow pastures. Brown barns and clusters of white-and-black-spotted dairy cows dotted the length of the valley.

"I like watching cows," said Mr. Popolo as he chomped into his sandwich. "They seem so content. Tiara won't be the same without them."

"Mr. Popolo, we're not taking them with us," said Bianca.

"I know that. I'm talking about the Wizard's plans," Mr. Popolo replied.

"He's going to get rid of our cows?" Bianca asked in disbelief.

"Well, most of them. He said we won't need the methane gas from their manure anymore. We'll burn wood and coal instead to heat our buildings. He said the coal is not doing any good in the ground," Mr. Popolo explained.

"But that would mean digging up the valley to get the coal," protested Lara. "And, we'd be choking on soot and smoke in the winter."

"Is that Neechie's idea of a modern Tiara?" Bianca said scornfully.

"Well, I don't know much about this kind of thing. But the Wizard says Tiara can't stay the way it is forever. We have to become part of the modern world," said Mr. Popolo.

"I like Tiara the way it is," Bianca fumed.

Lara changed the subject. "To get to Mrs. Arbor's house, we have to go up another hill and then into the forest for a ways," she said, looking sympathetically at Mr. Popolo. His huge body was more bulk than muscle, and it was not made for bicycling. "To continue past Mrs. Arbor's, we'll need horses," she added.

"I was thinking of that," said Mr. Popolo. "I can pick up some from Mr. Bovine's farm." He pointed to a road that sloped down the side of the hill, away from Mrs. Arbor's house.

"You go on ahead and I can catch up with you at Mrs. Arbor's," he suggested.

Bianca and Lara agreed, and Mr. Popolo quickly finished his lunch. He then gently settled down on his frail-looking bicycle and coasted down the road to Farmer Bovine's place.

Bianca and Lara continued on until they reached the top of the next hill, at the edge of the Tygan Forest.

The road plunged into a wall of tall oak trees. The sun was low on the horizon and shadows from the trees made the forest appear far darker than the valley below them.

The two girls dismounted and stood silently for awhile, looking back at Tiara. The town capped a low-lying hill on the other side of the valley. Sunlight reflected off the palace's red spires, which poked above the town's blue wall.

"It seems so small and distant," Bianca said in a hushed tone.

Lara swung her arm around Bianca's shoulders. "We don't have to go on. We can turn back if you want," she offered.

Bianca peered into the forest's darkness. The wind was picking up now. Leaves danced in the trees and a slight chill ran through her. Home and friends were being left behind for an adventure she had not sought. "We should go on. If I think about it too long, I might lose my nerve."

Without further talk, they got back on their bikes and entered a world of giant trees.

Sunlight poked through the branches, creating long ghostly beams that they passed through. Small lizards skittered across their path and birds swooped over their heads. Ahead of them, a deer leaped into the underbrush.

It was a slow advance. The paved brick road became a humble, dirt path. Their bikes no longer rolled atop a smooth surface; they now labored through loose dirt, large ruts and bulging tree roots.

"Mrs. Arbor's house isn't too far up this road. When we see a deep ravine we'll be very near. It's across the road from her house," said Lara.

Suddenly, Lara motioned Bianca to stop. She whispered, "I hear something odd in the background." Sentries always listened closely for Vandals. "Let's pull our bikes behind those bushes."

After they were hidden, Bianca asked impatiently, "What did you hear?" It would soon be dark and she didn't want to travel at night. Then, ever so faintly, she heard it herself. Soon the forest was engulfed in its roar.

They peered over the bushes. A helmeted rider on a black motorcycle raced past them, throwing stones and dirt off to the sides of the road.

"A Vandal!" exclaimed Bianca.

"I'm not sure. They usually ride in groups. But who else would have a motorcycle?" Lara wondered aloud.

"Let's get going. I want to get to Mrs. Arbor's as soon as possible. There could be others out here," said Bianca, pushing her bike back onto the path.

Soon the aroma of cookies filled the air and Mrs. Arbor's house appeared around the bend. It was a three-story stone mansion, with many windows, two turrets and a large porch. It was so old, no one could remember who built it.

Her day care had already closed for the evening, but Mrs. Arbor had ten children of her own, and they were playing outside.

Lara and Bianca rode up to the porch and set their bikes down. They were immediately surrounded by children, each demanding their attention.

Then Mrs. Arbor burst through her front door with a straw broom clenched between two well-defined, muscular hands. Her great bulk appeared ready to bust out of her gingham dress. With several broad sweeps of her broom, her children squealed and scattered off the porch.

"Quit this racket!" she commanded. "You'd better have your chores done before dinner, or I'll dunk your heads in a bucket of cold water."

Her gruff manner made Bianca step back. Lara assured her, "Mrs. Arbor has a way with young ones. They love her and live in fear of her as well. I've often heard her say 'There's a little bad in all of us that could use some punishment now and then.'"

"I bet she'd like Neechie," Bianca joked.

Mrs. Arbor came off the porch to look at her two new visitors. She recognized Lara immediately. "My, Lara, how you have grown. It's been six months since you've visited. You look even healthier and stronger than before."

Lara smiled and said, "Thanks, Mrs. Arbor. I work out every day."

"And who is your friend here? By her royal purple headband, I can see she's from the palace."

Bianca's glanced up, as if she could see her own headband. She didn't want it known she was from the palace. This darn thing has got to go, she thought, and quickly pulled it off.

It was too late. Lara said proudly, "This is Princess Bianca. King Kilian died two days ago and now Bianca is the ruler of the land."

Hating to be the center of attention, Bianca groaned, shuffled her feet and said "Hello."

"Well, she doesn't look so royal to me," Mrs. Arbor snapped. "But I'm sorry to hear that old King Kilian died. He was a good man. Then again, he was a man at that, so he did have his faults." She gave out a good belly-laugh.

"Why don't you rest in the waiting room with the other visitor till dinner." She motioned them to come in.

Lara asked, "What other visitor?"

"The guy that rode up on that," said Mrs. Arbor. She pointed to the side of her house: leaning against it was a black motorcycle.

CHAPTER 13

Surprise Guest

Inside Mrs. Arbor's waiting room, Bug leaned against a large oak table, munching a cookie. "Join me for cookies and milk?" he asked and laughed.

"What are you doing here?" said Bianca, both surprised and concerned. She set down her knapsack but kept an eye on him.

"You didn't think you could get away with stealing the Ruby Ring, did you?" Bug asked smugly. He snatched another cookie from a stack piled on the table next to him.

"I didn't steal it," Bianca hotly retorted. Luckily, the Ruby was still in the pouch, underneath her sweatshirt. Besides, how could he accuse her of theft? The Ruby Ring belonged to her, since she was the ruler of Tiara.

"You know what happens to little girls who lie, don't you?" Bug crushed the cookie in his fist and crumbs dropped to the floor.

Lara stepped beside Bianca. She was as tall as Bug. "Feeling tough? Because you've got a motorcycle?"

"Where did you get it? From a Vandal?" Bianca asked defiantly.

Bug snickered and gulped some milk. "I keep it hidden in the forest. And...," He grinned wickedly, "maybe I am a Vandal."

Bianca and Lara exchanged glances.

"Anyhow, things are going to change around here. There's going to be more excitement, more fun," said Bug, raising his glass for emphasis.

"What are you talking about? Neechie is always telling people to work harder," said Bianca.

"Well, some people should work harder. And, some should play more. Don't worry though. You won't be doing much of either," said Bug, smirking.

Bianca felt safe from Bug's threats. She only wished she

could read his mind. The Ruby Ring wasn't working.

"Cat got your tongue, Bianca?" Bug sneered and took a step toward her.

"No!" Bianca said firmly.

Lara stepped between Bug and Bianca. "What do you want?" she demanded.

Bug retreated and sat on the table. He knew Lara was a fighter. Peering at Bianca, he demanded, "Where's the Ruby Ring?"

"Why don't you just leave us alone," said Bianca and then she held up her hands. "You can see I'm not wearing it – stupid!" She was angry and, she realized, perhaps foolish for taunting Bug.

But he didn't respond; he seemed frustrated. He scratched a scab on his chin and looked Lara and Bianca up and down.

Mrs. Arbor marched into the room. "Lara, I've decorated the guest room upstairs. You must see it." She grabbed Lara by the arm.

"Bianca, join us," Lara said and drew her near. "It's best to come with us," she whispered.

"Do you think it's OK to leave him here?" Bianca whispered back.

"What harm can he do?" Lara said as they climbed the stairs.

When they entered the guest room, Bianca heard the motorcycle start up. "Is Bug leaving?" she asked and ran over to the window. Lara joined her.

Bug had his helmet on and was revving his motorcycle.

"He's taking our knapsacks!" Bianca cried.

"He must think the Ruby Ring is in one of them," said Lara.

"That's our supplies for the trip!" Bianca opened the window and yelled out, "Bug, stop! Bring our things back!"

He ignored her and wheeled his cycle around, toward the road.

By chance, Mr. Popolo was riding up on a horse with two others in tow. He leaned forward in his saddle as the motorcycle came directly toward him.

Bianca and Lara shouted from the house, "Mr. Popolo, stop him!"

Bug swerved to the side, but Mr. Popolo reacted quickly. He heaved his massive body off his horse and onto Bug's motorcycle.

A tremendous thud shook the ground. And then the sound of Bug's cycle crashing down the ravine and cries of pain echoed throughout the woods.

Mrs. Arbor's children raced out of the house, screaming and yelling, to see what had happened. Bianca and Lara followed close behind.

Concerned about Mr. Popolo, Bianca yelled down into the dark ravine, "Are you OK, Mr. Popolo?"

There was no reply. "We have to find him. He could be seriously hurt," said Lara.

Mrs. Arbor fetched a lantern from her house. Lara took it and edged down the ravine's steep side. Bianca followed in her footsteps to the bottom of the ravine where Mr. Popolo lay. Although initially suspicious of him, she now felt badly for doubting his loyalty.

Mr. Popolo's eyes were closed. His shirt and pants were ripped. Bianca nudged his huge arm with her hand, "Mr. Popolo, can you hear me?"

One eye opened, the other was swollen shut. He mumbled to Bianca, "Are you an angel?"

"No, Mr. Popolo. I'm Bianca. Don't you remember me?" She feared that he may have seriously injured his head.

"Oh, yes. It's coming back to me. I just tackled a Vandal," he said, holding his head.

"It was Bug and he was stealing our packs. Luckily they didn't roll down the ravine," she said.

"I guess I wasn't as lucky," said Mr. Popolo as he tried to get up. "Oops. I can't move my leg."

Lara felt it carefully. "You may have broken it." She looked back up the steep ravine and frowned. "It's too dark to get you up to the road."

"Don't worry about me. I'll be safe. I've camped out in this part of the forest before," Mr. Popolo said bravely.

"But we can't just leave you here," protested Bianca.

"Mrs. Arbor can give us some blankets for Mr. Popolo," said Lara.

"That'll be fine. It'll be just like camping in my younger days," he said.

"OK, we'll be right back. Then, first thing in the morning we'll get you to the top," Lara said.

Bianca and Lara soon returned from Mrs. Arbor's house with blankets, food and a spare lantern. Then they decided to look for Bug.

Carefully balancing themselves, they hopped from boulder to boulder till Lara spotted Bug's cycle. "This is a wreck. It won't be going anywhere," she said, pointing to the twisted frame.

"I don't see Bug anywhere and it's getting dark," Bianca said, glancing around.

"Soon it'll be impossible to find anything unless we're stepping on it," said Lara.

"Don't say that. It gives me the creeps. He could be dead," said Bianca.

"Or he might be alive and watching us," said Lara. "We should go back to Mrs. Arbor's house."

Bianca shook her head in agreement. "This place is getting creepy."

By the time they reached the road, Mrs. Arbor and her brood had gone inside. On the porch, Bianca stopped Lara and asked, "Do you think Bug is a Vandal?"

"I don't know. He certainly acted like one today," mused her friend.

"If he's alive, he may follow us into the forest," said Bianca.

Lara bit her lip. "And if he is a Vandal, he might not be alone next time."

Bianca considered this for a few seconds and said, "It's time we talk to Mrs. Arbor about asking the Wood Nymphs to help us." She then tilted her head slightly and asked, "Do you think they really exist?"

"We'll find out soon enough," Lara said softly, turning to look back on the ravine.

The forest's dark shadows had become a vast black canvas alive with the sounds of hundreds of creatures moving about.

"I just hope they don't turn us into mushrooms," said Bianca.

CHAPTER 14

Meeting Old Friends

L ara and Bianca walked into a dining room full of commotion. Mrs. Arbor's children were cleaning up after dinner, dragging their chairs across the wooden floor, heaping their dishes and silverware together, and shouting to each other across the room.

At first, neither Lara nor Bianca noticed the two children sitting at the far end of the long oak dining table. Then one of them stood up and yelled, "Bianca! It's me. Jewel!" Sitting beside her was Laser, biting into a drumstick.

"You made it! I knew you would." Bianca ran up and embraced Jewel.

Laser patted Bianca on the back. "I guess we got here too late to warn you about Bug. Mrs. Arbor told us what happened. But where's Bug?"

"We don't know. Maybe he's still in the ravine. We couldn't find him," said Bianca.

"I always thought Bug was creepy," said Jewel.

"Me, too. But I thought the Wizard was OK, even if he did brag a lot. Then we overhead him talking to Bug. He's dangerous," Laser said.

"What happened? How did you get here? Did your parents change their minds?" The questions tumbled out of Bianca.

"Jewel and I were watching you bike through the valley from your tower. Mom and Dad had just joined us when the Wizard and Bug walked onto the main balcony below," said Laser.

"Wizard pointed to the forest and said those logs would make them rich. And there was no one to stop them. He saw you leaving with your packs and figured you were trying to get to Zurbia. He laughed and said your leaving was the perfect solution. He could rule in your name forever!" Laser recounted.

Jewel chimed in, "The Wizard assumed that you had taken the Ruby Ring, so he sent Bug to get it. And, he told him, above all, to make sure you didn't get to Zurbia."

"Dad got really upset when he heard them talking," said Laser. "He raced downstairs and started arguing with the Wizard. Dad said he'd personally call a town council to take away the Wizard's powers."

Jewel added, "Mom went downstairs to calm Dad down. She thought he might punch the Wizard. We went down too, but stayed out of sight."

"When Mom got down there, she found Dad lying unconscious on the floor. I think Bug hit him from behind. But the Wizard said Dad slipped on the floor and hit his head," said Laser.

"I can't believe this. What did your mom do?" asked Lara.

"She was really upset. Bug had left before she got down there, so she started yelling at the Wizard. He then said Mom poisoned Rip," said Laser.

"No one would believe that," Bianca blurted out.

"The Wizard said Mom and Dad couldn't leave the palace and went to call the guards."

"As soon as the Wizard left, we raced over to Mom," said Jewel. "Dad came to and held his head. He said that the Wizard had to be stopped. Mom said they would be OK, but we had to warn you about Bug before the Wizard returned. She said that the future of Tiara depended on you."

"I'm not sure what we should do now," Laser said. "Bug might still be out there planning something. And if Mr. Popolo can't accompany you ..." He searched for words.

Lara leaned back in her chair and said, "I don't think it's safe for you to go back. The Wizard would just lock you up in the palace with your parents."

Jewel grew pale and more freckles appeared. Laser was unusually quiet.

Lara noted it was getting late and suggested that they talk

again in the morning. Laser and Jewel agreed and everyone headed upstairs to their rooms.

That night in bed Bianca thought about Neechie trying to stop her from reaching Zurbia: Attena had to be there. Now if she could only get past the Vandals and cross the Tygan Mountains...

CHAPTER 15

The Ways of the Nymphs

Bianca awoke early the next day and peered out the window. A thick fog hugged the ground. A white misty haze filled the air and seemed to swallow the trees, leaving only the near ones visible.

While the others slept, she tiptoed downstairs and stepped out on the porch. The fog seemed to slowly bubble out of the ravine, spilling over and onto the road, lapping right up to the house.

Suddenly something very large moved down by the road. Bianca could barely see its form. She rubbed her eyes to wipe the sleep out of them. Was she imagining things?

Bianca stepped off the porch and walked toward the main road leading up to the front yard. The fog slowly rolled and swirled around her as if she were plunging into a ghostly silent river.

A deep-sounding moan came from down the road, near the ravine. She stood still, not daring to move. If only the fog were a blanket that I could wrap around myself – then I would be invisible, she thought.

Again, she heard the moan. But it sounded sorrowful, not threatening. Bianca wavered between retreating back to the house and wading deeper into the fog.

"Who's out there?" she yelled. "Is someone hurt?"

There was no reply. She cautiously stepped closer to the source of the moaning. The sharp snap of twigs, breaking under her shoes, cracked the stillness around her.

One more time, she heard the moaning. Her heart beat faster. But still, she drew closer to the pathetic sound, instinctively responding to a call for help.

Finally, she glimpsed something emerging from the mist –something the size of a bear hugging the ground.

She held her breath and studied the hulk until she realized it was actually the body of a large man. "Is that you, Mr. Popolo?"

The shape moved slowly, rolling more than rising.

"Yes it is," came a weak reply.

"Are you OK?" Bianca asked as she ran toward him.

"Well I'm pretty sore all over. I still can't move my leg."

"How did you get up the ravine? Did someone help you?" Bianca bent over to examine him more closely.

Mr. Popolo scratched his thick curly hair and then stared at her. "I really don't know. I just woke up now. I don't know who could've helped me."

"It was the Wood Nymphs," came a gruff voice from behind Bianca.

Surprised by the voice, Bianca leaped up and turned around to see Mrs. Arbor.

"They're out there," Mrs. Arbor said, pointing toward the fog-covered ravine. "They live throughout the woods, and they rule it more certainly than any king or queen ever ruled Tiara."

"Then they really do exist. They helped Mr. Popolo up the ravine. So, they must be friendly," Bianca said hopefully.

"They're friendly to those who do good. But anyone harming the forest may spend eternity as a mushroom," cautioned Mrs. Arbor.

"How do you harm the forest?" Bianca asked.

"Needlessly killing animals or cutting down trees, and, of course, littering. The Vandals drop their beer bottles all over the forest," she said. And then she added with a hearty laugh, "Many of them are now mushrooms."

Just as Mrs. Arbor finished, Laser and Jewel came running toward them. The fog had now lifted between the road and the house.

"Wow, Mr. Popolo, you look pretty bad," said Jewel.

"How did you get up here? I thought you had a broken leg," asked Laser.

"The Wood Nymphs brought him up," said Bianca. She felt

a little smug knowing something Laser didn't.

"I don't see Bug anywhere, I guess they didn't bother with him," said Laser, looking around the edge of the ravine.

"It's still too foggy down there to see anything," said Jewel.

"Don't worry. I'll organize a search for him after the ravine clears up," said Mrs. Arbor.

A moment later, Lara and Mrs. Arbor's children joined them and helped lift Mr. Popolo onto a wooden trailer that they pulled to the house. After a "heave-ho", they planted him on a large porch swing.

"I guess I'm not going to be able to travel very far," Mr. Popolo said, scratching his head. "The Wood Nymphs can't carry me all the way to Zurbia. I'm sorry, Bianca, but I won't be able to go with you," he apologized.

"We have to go on but I promise that we'll return before your leg has healed," she said bravely, but more aware now of the dangers that she and Lara faced without Mr. Popolo's help.

Laser awkwardly shuffled forward. "Bianca. I want to go with you and Lara. I can be helpful and ... hey, I won't cause any problems."

Bianca didn't mind if Laser joined them, as long as he didn't try to boss her around. He seemed sincere and he obviously was looking forward to the adventure. Bianca glanced at Lara, who gave her the thumbs up sign.

"OK. You can come with us," Bianca said.

Laser slapped her on the back. "Bianca you made the right decision!"

Jewel looked at Laser, Lara and Bianca. She stuck her hands in her jeans' pockets and said, "I want to go too and I know we should go now. But still ..." She looked around at the others as if mentally calculating their chance of success.

"Sis, just stay here with Mr. Popolo. We don't want to baby sit you."

Jewel's hands flew out of her pockets, forming fists. "Oh, yeah! Well, I can take care of myself, Mr. Know-it-all."

"Maybe you should stay here..." Lara began, but Jewel interrupted her.

"You don't believe I can take care of myself, either. You think I'd be a burden. What about you, Bianca?"

Bianca thought for a moment. Did she want to place Jewel in danger? And yet Jewel was her buddy – she couldn't leave her behind. "You can do it," said Bianca.

Jewel smiled. They were still loyal friends. "OK, I'm going." With raised eyebrows, she added, "I just hope we don't run into any Vandals."

Bianca and Lara laughed. "Don't worry, the Wood Nymphs will help us," said Bianca.

"By the way, who are these Wood Nymphs?" Laser asked skeptically.

"I can tell you all about them at breakfast," Mrs. Arbor said. "Then you can be off. You should make it to the Last Inn before nightfall. That's the last outpost of greater Tiara before you head into the mountains."

At breakfast, Mrs. Arbor described the owner of the Last Inn. His name was Backus and he was the only person she knew who actually got along with the Vandals. They sometimes visited his inn when they came over the Tygan Mountains.

She said Mr. Backus kept the inn open to all travelers, offering them all the same food and shelter. Although he could be wild at times, overall, she felt he was more foolhardy than dangerous. But she cautioned, "Keep an eye on him."

Mrs. Arbor's guests had become very quiet. She chortled and said, "Oh, I forgot to mention that Backus has some great video games. In fact, that's why the Vandals often visit him."

"Terrific, I love video games," said Laser. Tiara had only one video parlor and it was usually too crowded to give him a chance to play.

After hearing about the Wizard's plans for Tiara, she offered to help them on their mission. She packed them sandwiches, supplied Jewel and Laser with blankets and extra clothes, and asked one of her sons to bring them an additional horse from her stable.

Bianca and her friends thanked Mrs. Arbor for her generosity. Mr. Popolo shook their hands from his swing and told them to be careful. Mrs. Arbor would take care of him until he was able to walk again.

But when her son returned with a horse, he had some bad news. "Mom, someone broke into the stable last night and stole a horse."

"That's never happened before," said Mrs. Arbor. "Who would have done that?"

"Maybe a Vandal," Bianca suggested.

"Not likely. They prefer motorcycles," said Mrs. Arbor.

"Unless they don't have one," said Lara looking toward the ravine where she and Bianca had found Bug's wrecked motorcycle. "I think Bug got out of the ravine."

CHAPTER 16

The Last Inn

The morning ride to the Last Inn was shrouded in mist. When it lifted, Bianca found herself in a forest carpeted with large ferns. A thick blanket of low-lying clouds blocked out the sun, muting the forest colors into endless shades of green. Lunch was eaten on a moss-covered stream bank, near a waterfall.

"This trip is pretty easy," said Jewel. "All I've seen are birds and squirrels, not one dangerous animal."

"Well they've got their eyes on you," Laser said.

Lara shot him a dirty look. "Don't listen to your brother. We'll do fine. Of course, if Laser doesn't pick up his trash after lunch, he could wake up as a mushroom."

Bianca lay on the ground listening to the others while she stared up at the long thin pine trees, swaying gently in the breeze.

"I don't think Bug could ever find us," Bianca said, feeling safe under the giant canopy of fine pine needles.

"I'll feel safer once we reach this Last Inn. I'm more worried about the Vandals than any dangerous animals," said Jewel, getting up and walking toward her horse.

The others followed her and soon they were galloping down the road toward the Last Inn.

After what seemed to be many, long hours, the road turned onto a bluff where they stopped to take in the view. About half a mile away and below them was a two-story log cabin in a clearing. Dozens of large ravens circled the low sky above it. Their shrill squawks pierced the quiet.

"That must be it," said Bianca. The last inn before the long journey up the Tygans.

"It's a lot smaller than Mrs. Arbor's house, and I bet they

don't have showers," Jewel said, scratching the back of her neck.

They trotted down the winding road and within a short time came to a field of low grass. The Last Inn was at the far end, tall evergreens towered right behind it.

The inn's wooden sign dangled unevenly by one wire over its small porch. The building looked abandoned. There were no horses or motorcycles out front.

"Do you think anyone's around?" Jewel asked.

"Only one way to find out," said Laser. "Let's go in."

They dismounted and Lara led the way. The front door was slightly ajar. Lara knocked on it. There was no answer. She grasped the knob and pushed the door wide open.

Inside were eight oak tables spread out in a large room. A long smooth oak counter ran across the length of the back. On the back wall hung a huge mirror. Just to the left of the entrance was a "Space Invaders" video game.

"I don't know about the rest of you, but I'm playing 'Space Invaders'," said Laser. He slid onto a stool in front of the game, slipped in a coin and began firing away.

The game made two sounds: a small explosion every time Laser scored a direct hit on an enemy spacecraft and a high-pitched whistling sound every time he fired and missed.

A deep voice boomed out from the back of the room. "Hey, buddy. What do you think you're doing?"

Frightened, Laser jumped from the stool and whipped around from the game.

A large, barrel-chested man with a stubbly beard stood behind the counter. Although he had thick, wavy red hair, the wall mirror behind him revealed a perfectly round bald spot. He wore a soiled T-shirt that read "I Eat Small Animals."

Bianca whispered to Lara, "It's a good thing we're not small animals."

CHAPTER 17

Mr. Backus

"I said, 'What are you doing buddy?'" The stranger growled even louder than before.

Laser stood motionless. His lips moved slightly as if about to answer but nothing came out.

Lara spoke out, "Are you Mr. Backus? We're traveling through and Mrs. Arbor suggested that we spend the night here."

"Traveling through? To where?" He shot back, lifting his right hand to reveal an unlit, stubby cigar. "By the way, any of you got a match?" He pointed to the cigar with his other hand.

Laser found his voice. "Yes, sir. I have one." He reached into his gadget belt and pulled up a small lighter.

"Well, bring it here, kid," the man ordered.

Unsteadily, Laser walked toward him. He raised his arm and offered his lighter.

A large, fleshy hand, swallowed the lighter. He lit his cigar, inhaled deeply, blew out some smoke and said, "I am Mr. Backus."

He took another draw on his cigar and then released a second billowing cloud. "Whom are you?" His voice filled the room.

Jewel spoke up from behind Lara and Bianca, "It's who are you? Not whom are you?"

"What do we have here? Little Miss Proper Grammarian? Step forward, sweetie," Mr. Backus bellowed.

Jewel did not move. Her face went pale, freckles exploded across her face.

"I said move!" Mr. Backus roared.

Jewel tiptoed around Lara and Bianca and squeaked "Hello."

With a deep laugh, Mr. Backus replied, "Hello, indeed!"

Jewel responded with a timid laugh.

The two kept laughing until Mr. Backus wound down to a low rumble. After taking a puff on his cigar, he blew out a particularly foul-smelling cloud.

Jewel wrinkled her nose in disgust.

Bianca feared the worst from Mr. Backus. But instead of snarling at them again, he said, "You must be hungry after riding all the way from Mrs. Arbor's. Sit down and I'll fix you some grub."

Bianca looked at Lara apprehensively. Lara said, "I think it's OK. And I'm hungry."

Jewel, Bianca and Lara cautiously sat down at a nearby table. Laser slowly backed away from the innkeeper and joined them.

Mr. Backus opened a door behind the counter and entered what appeared to be a kitchen. After he had left the room, Bianca asked the others, "What do you think? He seems weird to me."

"I think so too," said Lara. "I'm not sure if we should spend the night here or camp out."

"Outside?" asked Jewel nervously, glancing out the window.

Mr. Backus returned with some bowls of stew. On a separate silver tray he served bread and cheese. After a long day on the road, the hot stew tasted great. Mr. Backus swept a towel back and forth across the counter top, eyeing them while they ate.

When Laser finished his stew, he returned to "Space Invaders". Jewel stood looking over his shoulder, impatiently waiting to play. Lara and Bianca sat at the table, talking to each other.

"Hey, the kid wearing a purple headband is from Tiara's palace, isn't she?" Mr. Backus called to Bianca and Lara above the explosions and whistles of the video game. His eyes were fixed on Jewel.

Bianca leaned over to Lara and said softly, "I should have told Jewel not to wear her headband."

"I think she picked it up at a yard sale," said Lara.

"Yard sale! Not likely," Mr. Backus said bluntly. "From what I hear, only those living in the palace wear them."

Cupping his hands around his mouth, he yelled to Jewel, "Hey! Are you that Princess Bianca?"

Bianca stiffened. Jewel didn't hear him, though. She was shooting down alien ships and squealing, "I'm beating you! I'm beating you!"

Laser yelled back, "You cheated! You cheated!" He grabbed the silver tray that had held the bread and cheese. "You think you're good at games. Try finding this." Laser threw the tray out the front door. It spun like a Frisbee into the woods.

Lara immediately jumped up. "Laser, that was unnecessary."

Bianca saw a chance to get off alone and take out the Ruby Ring. She headed to the restroom, as Mr. Backus stepped around the far side of the counter. Anger turned his face as red as a cherry. "You kids think you're Vandals, huh? You better find that tray right now, or I'll hand you over to real Vandals."

Jewel and Lara dashed outside to find the tray. With hands in his pockets, Laser reluctantly followed them at his own pace.

Shutting the restroom door behind her, Bianca slid the leather cord from around her neck. She opened the pouch and dropped the Ruby Ring into her hand.

I don't understand, she thought. The ring worked when Neechie was in my room but it hasn't worked since. I've got to find out what Mr. Backus is up to.

She fingered the Ruby Ring in her palm and heard a roaring sound. At first it seemed to be some magical powers coming from the ring. But no, it was the sound of motorcycles.

Bianca cracked open the door and peered out. Mr. Backus was alone, looking out the front door. He yelled, "Now you'll meet some real Vandals."

His huge body filled the doorway, blocking her view. But through the paneled windows she saw black motorcycles.

Her heart stopped. She was trapped.

CHAPTER 18

Vandals

Bianca gently closed the restroom door and locked it. She glanced around the small room. There was no window to crawl through.

The Vandals talked outside. "Hey Buck, what gives with these horses. You got guests?"

"Yeah, I think we got ourselves that princess from Tiara," said Mr. Backus.

"Bug was right. She was coming this way," said a Vandal.

"Yeah, Bug said the shorter one was the princess, but there were more than two kids. I still recognized her though. She was wearing that purple headband only kids from the palace wear."

"Are they inside?" A Vandal asked.

"No. They're out in the underbrush, looking for a tray the boy threw out there."

Another yelled out, "Sounds like young Vandals to me." Laughter followed.

Bianca hoped her friends were safe outside. They think Jewel is me, she thought. They're probably after the Ruby Ring.

"How about a little wine, Backus, before we rustle them up," said one of the Vandals, followed by the sounds of heavy boots stomping into the inn.

Bianca crossed her fingers, hoping Mr. Backus hadn't noticed that she had gone to the restroom.

"Bug said she had the Ruby Ring, right? And that the Wizard would reward us if we got it to him?" asked one of the Vandals, stomping into the inn.

Another Vandal spoke. "Too bad about Bug's nasty accident." They all laughed again.

Mr. Backus said, "That boy was just too uppity. I told him, 'Bug, we wanna talk directly to the Wizard, not just through you.' But no, he had to be a big shot. He got what he deserved."

There was a round of "Yeahs!" and "That's right!"

Bianca shuddered at what they might have done to Bug.

"Ever since you guys got rid of those messengers from Attena, all the Wizard can think about is getting control of Tiara," said Mr. Backus.

Bianca now realized that no one had heard from Attena because the Vandals had killed her messengers.

The Vandals continued talking loudly. "Well, if he builds that road from Zurbia, he'll make a fortune," said a Vandal.

"And we'll get rich," another added in a harsh, guttural voice.

They're talking about Neechie's plan to cut down the Tygan Forest, she thought.

Mr. Backus told his visitors they should round up the kids because it was getting dark.

Bianca prayed that all of them would go outside. Then she could run to the back of the inn, and if lucky, find a rear door that opened to the forest. She fingered the Ruby Ring still in her hand. It was too dangerous keeping it out. She stuffed it back in the pouch.

Bianca unlocked the door and opened it just a sliver to peek out. About six dark-haired men, dressed from head to toe in black leather, stood around drinking from wine bottles. Shiny metal studs trailed down the length of their jacket sleeves. Their tall black boots had pointed toes with steel tips.

As they walked to the front door, one of the Vandals asked Mr. Backus, "How many kids are we looking for? There are four horses. So I suppose four, huh?"

Mr. Backus scratched his fat cheek with the same hand that held his cigar. "Let me see. That's right. There were four."

Bianca's heart skipped a beat.

"But I remember only three of them running outside." He turned his head to look over the entire room. His eyes swept past her door.

Bianca prayed, "Please, don't let them find me."

Just then the silver tray that Laser had thrown, sailed threw the open door. It struck one of the Vandals in the head. Bianca heard Laser yell from outside, "Vandals smell like puke."

The injured Vandal cursed loudly and all of them rushed out of the inn. A motorcycle engine whined loudly amidst a chorus of shouts.

It was now or never. She flung open the door.

CHAPTER 19

Becoming the Hunted

Bianca dashed to the back of the inn. But in her flight she failed to notice Mr. Backus standing in her path. She bounced off him and fell backwards to the floor. He looked as surprised as she felt.

She rolled backwards onto her feet, stood up and darted around Mr. Backus. With two leaps she was at the counter. She planted her hands on its top and was about to swing her legs over.

Mr. Backus yelled "Hey, there's one in here!" He reached out, barely catching Bianca's sleeve just as her legs were arching over the counter. A second later, she would have been free.

As it was, her legs came crashing down on the counter top. and her arm was pinned to it by Mr. Backus's hand. He twisted her sleeve, cutting into her arm. "Stop it, you're hurting me," she yelled.

Backus laughed, "Looks like I got myself a real prize. Hey! Do you live in the palace, too?" He loosed his grip just a bit. She managed to swing her feet back down to the ground so she could stand up.

Bianca stopped struggling. It was no use fighting him: he was too big. She had to think real hard. I've got to trick him into releasing me, she told herself.

"Look, I've got something very valuable. If you let me go I'll give it to you. If you don't let me go, you'll have to share it with the Vandals."

"Hmm. So let's make a deal, huh?" Mr. Backus said. He took a long draw on his cigar.

Bianca anxiously glanced at the front door. The Vandals might return at any moment.

"So what do you have?" Backus asked gruffly.

"I've got Tiara's Ruby Ring."

"You've got it! That's pretty tricky. That princess had you carry it. Well, where is it?" he demanded.

"I hid it in the restroom. I was going to come back for it later."

"Take me to it," Mr. Backus barked, pushing her toward the restroom, while still gripping her sleeve.

When Bianca reached the room, she glanced around for a likely place she could have hidden it. She pointed to a loose wooden plank at the far corner of the small room. "It's right under there. I dropped it under that plank. But I can't lift it."

She looked into his eyes and said boldly, "You can do it, unless you want your Vandal friends to help you."

Mr. Backus squinted at the wooden plank and scratched his chin. "OK. Come along."

With a firm grip on her, he dragged her to the spot. Bending over, he tried to lift the plank with one hand. It moved slightly. Bianca held her breath. Would he discover he had been tricked?

Mr. Backus grunted and groaned. The plank didn't give. He cursed and dropped to his knees to use both hands. For just a second, he let go of her sleeve.

Bianca bolted out of the room, slamming the door behind her. She heard a crashing sound and then some swearing. No time to look behind, she thought, and sprinted to the back of the counter and straight-armed a swinging door.

She burst into the kitchen and saw an exit door at the back. She skirted a cutting table to closely, knocking off several pots and pans and splattering stew all over the floor. Her foot slipped on it and she slid into a pantry shelf, causing flour and sugar to dump out, just missing her.

Suddenly the floor began to shake. Mr. Backus's heavy panting filled the room as he charged into it.

She reached the door, grabbed the knob, twisted it hard and hoped it was unlocked. The door swung open revealing a six-foot drop to the ground. She jumped, hit the earth, rolled over several times and sprang to her feet.

Don't look behind, just run, she thought. Head for the thickest underbrush. As she raced, thistles scrapped her skin, thorns tore at her clothes and branches jabbed her sides and legs. Behind her the whining scream of motorcycles sliced through the evening air.

As night fell, shadows crisscrossed shadows, forming a patchwork of dark, eerie images. Like a deer escaping hunters, Bianca blended into the maze of dark, strange shapes for protection. Eventually she reached a small clearing surrounded by tall pine trees, their trunks barely visible in the darkness.

Breathing heavily, she stood still and listened to the sounds around her. Bats darted overhead, a small animal rustled across some nearby leaves and something else, perhaps a wolf, howled in the distance. But she heard no motorcycles. She had escaped the Vandals.

For the first time, Bianca was alone in the forest. She huddled next to a log, exhausted from running. She had no idea where she was, except that it was a far stranger land than her town.

If only I could stay calm, everything will work out she thought. In the morning, I'll search for my friends. "Nothing to be afraid of. Nothing to be afraid of," she chanted softly. Despite her fear, she was exhausted and her eyelids began to close.

Just as she was about to drift off, something made her bolt upright. Had something moved? It was too dark to see. Have to be on guard, she thought. The Vandals might be near.

But her resolve to stay awake failed and she drifted into sleep – just as the rustling of leaves and the snapping of twigs grew louder around her.

CHAPTER 20

Wood Nymphs

W hen Bianca awoke, the morning sun was warming her face. She had slept soundly and had been kept warm and dry under a layer of moss. It's almost as if it had been placed it over me, she thought.

She propped herself up on her right elbow and studied the forest. Shafts of bright sunlight streaked through the tall pines. Dewdrops glistened, clinging to ferns like jewels, and bird screeched from some hidden perch overhead. Two others chased each other among the treetops.

What a beautiful place. Why don't the Vandals appreciate it, she mused. And how could Neechie want to cut it down? Just let the forest be itself.

A twig snapped just then and she glanced around nervously. The pine trees gently swayed, the dew sparkled and the birds flew over head. Nothing seemed different.

But out of the corner of her eye, she saw, or thought she saw, some people standing just beyond a thin veil of light. She rubbed her eyes. When she looked again, there were only trees and ferns.

Bianca sensed she was being watched, and although it made her feel uncomfortable, she somehow wasn't frightened.

"Who's out there? Please come out so I can see you," she called out, trying to sound casual.

Then, right before her eyes, the trees shimmered in the mist, their trunks divided into legs, their branches formed arms, and their leaves became hair. What had been trees were now three young women. They looked slightly older than Lara, but it was hard to tell because each resembled a type of tree.

One had bright gray-blue spiked hair like a spruce. Another had fine green hair similar to pine needles. The third one had shaggy brown hair like the moss that clung to the maples. Their entire bodies were patterned with the colors of the trees from which they had just emerged.

"Are you Wood Nymphs?" Bianca asked, astonished by their appearance.

"We are who you think we are," said the nearest one, with the spiked gray-blue hair.

Bianca ran her fingers through her hair and wished it wasn't so tangled. She wanted to look nice for her first meeting with the Wood Nymphs, and she was a Princess. "My name is Bianca. I'm from Tiara."

"Princess Bianca," corrected the nymph.

"How did you know?" Bianca asked, surprised at having been identified. She jerked her hand to the top of her head, making sure the purple headband was gone.

"We know everything you think," the nymph replied.

How could they? Unless, they took my Ruby, Bianca wondered. She quickly placed her hand over her chest and felt the leather bag with the Ruby Ring in it.

The pine nymph turned to the other two and said, "She has a ruby, too!"

Bianca studied them closely. Two of them each wore a single pierced ruby earring, similar to her ruby.

Bianca felt odd, knowing that they could hear everything she thought. She remembered what Neechie had done when she was reading his mind. "Ohm, Ohm, Ohm," she chanted over and over again.

The Wood Nymphs were amused. The spruce nymph started giggling. She cupped her hand over her mouth to stop and asked, "Who taught you that cheap trick?"

"I learned it from the Wizard of Tiara," Bianca said sheepishly.

The Wood Nymphs looked at each other as though they knew who he was.

The maple nymph, who was smaller than the other two, asked, "Are you a friend of his?"

"No ..." Bianca hesitated, then sighed and said "I might as well tell you everything. I'm on a mission. It's all happened so suddenly... I didn't know I'd be on one until my father was poisoned."

Bianca briefly told them her story. She began from the day her father was crowned King to the previous evening's escape from the Vandals.

"That is some adventure!" said the maple nymph. "And you still have more ahead of you."

"I'd rather be at home playing," said Bianca wistfully. But she immediately felt silly. Playing make-believe games was not as important as finding her Mom and saving Tiara. On the other hand, she would like things to be back to normal.

"We saw someone who looked like a Wizard traveling to Tiara last year," said the spruce nymph. "He had a long white beard and a white robe. I remember because they were blowing in the wind when he rode by in a motorcycle's sidecar."

"That must have been him," said Bianca. "He told us that he used his magic to get the Vandals to take him to Tiara. Do you think he knows magic?"

"There are many kinds of magic: strong and weak, good and evil, real and phony. The Wizard knew enough to fool the Vandals. What do you think of his magic?" asked the spiked hair, spruce nymph.

"I know that he's cold hearted and I think his magic is phony," said Bianca, absent-mindedly kicking the earth.

"Then you shouldn't have any difficulty defeating him," replied the nymph. "Real magic comes from one's heart. Its power comes from the ancient bond between life and nature. Their harmony brings the warmth of love and sunlight, and their disharmony brings hate and darkness. With magic, a community can resist those that would destroy that harmony."

She then introduced herself as Selene. "This is Echo," she said pointing to the nymph that had been a pine. "And this is Pyx," she said of the smallest. "We should take Bianca to our home and give her something to eat," she told her companions.

"Thanks for the invitation but first I have to find my friends. Have you seen them?" Bianca asked hopefully.

Selene answered, "Are they the ones you referred to in your story as Lara, Jewel and Laser?"

"Yes," said Bianca, hoping that the nymphs would help her find them.

Pyx let out a long, low whistle. "Bad news, Bianca. We got 'shroom' happy and ..." She stole a glance at the other two nymphs to see if they were going to say anything. They didn't. So she went on, "...we turned them into mushrooms."

"You're kidding?" said Bianca with disbelief. She had often heard that Wood Nymphs could change people into mushrooms, but she never thought it would actually happen to her best friends.

"She's not joking," said Selene. "We didn't intend to turn them into mushrooms. Unfortunately there was too much commotion with the Vandals running their cycles through the woods and everyone throwing rocks at each other. It was just easier to shroom everyone."

"So, how do you change them back?" Bianca asked.

"That does present a problem," said Pyx. "We can't."

CHAPTER 21

Danger Ahead: Zurbia

Bianca couldn't imagine going on without her friends. Angry tears burned down her cheeks. "Why can't you make them normal again? You, you stupid trees," she shouted, glaring at them. Her own intensity surprised her.

The nymphs stared back at her with blank faces. Bianca wondered if they might change her into a mushroom next.

After a long pause, Selene said, "Only you can bring your friends back. It has to do with the power of memories to change the future. The strength of friendship to overcome hardships."

She smiled and then turned and walked away. The other nymphs followed her. Bianca was left wondering what to do, when Pyx looked back at her and called, "Come on."

Bianca caught up with them and walked, ill-tempered, beside Pyx.

"It's too bad that you have to visit Zurbia," Pyx said sadly.

Bianca asked absent-mindedly, still thinking about her friends, "Why's that?"

"It stinks!" said Pyx.

"It's worse than that. It's full of poisons," said Echo.

"Is it really that bad?" asked Bianca.

Selene nodded and said, "Wood Nymphs left the other side of the Tygan Mountains many years ago. People just destroyed the forests. They cut the healthiest trees down to use for building or to burn for fuel. And then they dug up the ground beneath them to get coal and burn it for fuel. The trees left standing are now dying because of acid rain."

"Acid rain?" asked Bianca.

"Yes, it's real. It strips the trees of their bark and needles or leaves. It would eat away our skin, too," said Selene.

Bianca scratched her head in thought, hoping her hair

wouldn't fall out when she visited Zurbia.

"It won't," said Selene. "At least not right away. But over the years, the acid rain and pollution will rot you."

"What? Will my fingers fall off?" Bianca looked at her hands trying to imagine how they would appear with a couple of fingers missing.

"No. The first thing to go are your dreams, then your imagination and finally your spirit," continued Selene. "The rotting takes place slowly. A little bit disappears each day. Until just the body remains and its desire to possess things."

"Possess things? I don't understand," said Bianca.

"Look at the Vandals. They are the result of Zurbia's conquest over nature. They are caught in an unnatural and endless cycle of desiring things, consuming them and then throwing them away to search for new things to possess.

"In nature, a thing of beauty and desire forms slowly. But too slowly for the people of Zurbia. They are addicted to speed, to wanting things as soon as they see them. They cut up the day into hours, then minutes, and then seconds. Every moment of the day is used for getting something. They cannot afford the time to appreciate clouds drifting across the sky, trees gently swaying in a breeze, buds emerging in spring and leaves falling in the autumn."

Bianca thought of Neechie and how he insisted that the people of Tiara work harder and faster. He couldn't understand why they didn't want to earn more money and own more things.

Selene continued, "People in Zurbia ignore their children because they spend all their time working to buy things. Eventually the children become Vandals, cruel toward others and, like their parents, concerned only with having their own needs met."

"I know how cruel they can be," said Bianca. "Some burned down my friend's house and killed her parents."

"Only once did we ever meet one that was different."

"What was he like?" asked Bianca.

"He saved Pyx's life," said Selene.

"It's true. About eight years ago I was sleeping late one morning when a bunch of Vandals came crashing through the forest. Two almost rode right over me. I was about to change into a tree when four more appeared right in front of me. I was so frightened, I ran."

"She should never have run," said Echo disapprovingly.

"I could have taken care of them, but I panicked and ran. I lost three of them in the woods, but the fourth followed me right up to a cliff," Pyx recalled.

Looking at Bianca seriously, Pyx said, "Nymphs can't fly, you know."

She continued on, "I thought for sure I'd be dead firewood. The other Vandals were nearby. He could have called out to them, but he didn't. He had a sad face. I could tell that his heart hadn't turned to stone yet."

"We stared at each other. The other Vandals were getting closer. Then he turned around and yelled out, 'She's not here; let's get back on the road.'"

"Then Pyx did a really stupid thing," interrupted Echo.

"I did not! I was just thankful that's all."

"What did you do?" asked Bianca curiously.

"She did something she shouldn't have," said Selene, firmly.

Bianca was more curious than ever. "What did you do?" she pressed.

Pyx looked away. Selene quickly changed the subject. She raised her arm and pointed to a grove of cedar trees. "Let's sit over there and eat. Afterward, you can find your friends."

Bianca was confused. What could they be talking about? She decided to pursue her questioning another time, for now she was most intent on finding her friends.

At the grove, they met a few more Wood Nymphs, who also resembled different types of trees. A large salad was served. Because she had not eaten since last night, Bianca's stomach growled for food. Nevertheless, she carefully moved the mushrooms to the side of her plate. Bianca couldn't help but wonder if any may have previously been something other than a mushroom.

While eating, one of the Nymphs would occasionally laugh for no apparent reason. Bianca thought their behavior odd until it occurred to her that they were reading each other's thoughts.

She noticed that each, except Pyx, wore a single ruby earring and a feeling of jealousy overcame her. How come their rubies work and mine doesn't, she thought, pouting.

Echo sat down beside her and asked, "Where is your Ruby? Why aren't you wearing it?"

"I can't. It doesn't fit my finger." Bianca took off the leather pouch and took out the Ruby Ring. The rest of the nymphs stopped talking.

Selene came over and stared down at her ring. "It's a very old and beautiful ring. I haven't seen one like that for at least a couple hundred years."

"You mean..." Bianca didn't finish her sentence. She carefully looked at Selene's smooth face. "You mean you're 200 hundred years old? You're older than my grandpa, King Kilian? But you don't look much older than my friend Lara and she's fifteen."

All the nymphs laughed. "Well I guess the outdoors does wonders for our skin," joked Selene.

"In any case, if you want your ruby to work, it must touch your skin. That's why we all wear our rubies in our ears. Of course, a finger ring would also work," said Selene.

"I didn't know that. No one showed me how it worked," said Bianca, sliding the ring on. But she heard only broken sentences in her mind. "What's wrong with it?" She asked Selene.

"The ring fits too loosely, so you're not getting good contact with it. You'd be better off with a new, smaller band or holding it in your hand," Selene explained.

"Or wearing it as an earring," said Pyx. Bianca wondered why Pyx was the only nymph without one.

"I understand now!" said Bianca. "I could hear Neechie's thoughts in my room because I was holding the ring in my hand. Later on I couldn't hear anyone's thoughts because the ruby was in the leather bag."

"That's right," said Selene. "And now it's time to find your friends with your Ruby Ring."

"How?" asked Bianca.

"Look over there," Selene said, pointing to the other side of the grove.

Bianca walked over and saw a large open field in front of her.

"I don't see anyone," she said disappointedly.

"Look down," said Selene.

There at her feet and throughout the field were mushrooms, thousands of them. She turned to ask what this meant. But, the nymphs had disappeared.

CHAPTER 22

Mushroom Hunting

Bianca sat on the ground, cross-legged, head cradled in the palms of her hands and facing a sea of round mushroom caps. What am I supposed to do now? she wondered.

The Ruby Ring was still around her finger and felt warm against her cheek. Selene wanted me to use the Ruby to find my friends. But how? I don't hear anything. Maybe I'm not holding it tight enough.

Bianca slipped the ring off her finger and squeezed it in her fist. But still she could hear no thoughts. Jewel and the others must be here somewhere, she thought, scanning field's thousand white dots.

She reached out and touched one of the mushrooms. "Hello. It's me, Bianca." It felt silly talking to a mushroom, but then again it wasn't any more unusual than talking and eating with Wood Nymphs.

Although the mushroom didn't say a word, she did hear it snoring.

Bianca touched another one and another one. They were all snoring. This is getting me nowhere! She fumed and stomped the ground. After a long sigh, she slowly started walking through the field. When she reached the center of it, Bianca stooped and touched one of the mushrooms.

It wasn't snoring. It was humming a song. Surprised, Bianca jerked back her finger. She touched it again and asked, "Who are you?"

"Who said that? Are you a nymph?" asked the mushroom.

"No I'm a princess. Who are you?" Bianca asked again.

"I'm a fourth-grade teacher. At least I was. I'm a mushroom now."

"How did that happen?" Bianca asked curiously.

"Well, I led my class into the woods for a field trip. We picnicked at a stream and afterward I didn't pick up their litter. In fact, I left a bundle of trash myself."

"And the nymphs turned you into a mushroom?" Bianca asked.

"And my class as well," the mushroom replied.

"I'm really sorry," said Bianca.

"I'm not," said the mushroom. "It's more peaceful being a mushroom in the forest than a fourth-grade teacher. And I feel just as appreciated."

Throughout the day, Bianca talked to many mushrooms that had formerly walked the earth as people. Most had become quite attached to the forest. Even those who had once been violent Vandals were now mellow mushrooms. But the task of finding her friends appeared hopeless.

When she reached the other end of the huge field, she collapsed like a rag doll. "I've been wandering around and around all day in this field, I'm not even sure where I started," Bianca muttered to herself. "I should give up and become a mushroom, at least no one would be chasing me."

Exhausted and aching from stooping over all day, Bianca curled up and fell asleep. Or did she? Ever so faintly a violin played a tune in the distance, it was the same one that Lara had played the night Bianca had visited her in Tiara.

The music became ever louder. Then right before her, a giant red ribbon floated above the ground like a sidewalk, pulsating in time with the music. It stretched on and on through the forest, wrapping around trees and bushes and arching over brooks and logs.

Bianca floated up to the ribbon and found herself skipping on it in time with the music. The forest became an orchestra, with every tree, a Wood Nymph playing a violin.

The tune became ever louder and faster. With long strides, Bianca ran to keep up as everything became a blur. Bianca's hair flew behind her like a kite's tail. On and on she ran in a frenzy, until she tumbled off the ribbon, head over heels, on to a large field of daisies.

Bianca awoke in the morning to find herself surrounded by those same daisies. Am I still dreaming? She pinched herself, and then noticed the Ruby Ring around her finger.

This is very odd, she thought. I don't remember putting it on. She slid the ring off and grasped it in her fist. But the field of mushrooms had been replaced by a field of daisies. How would she find her friends now?

Then she spotted three mushrooms nearby. Bianca reached out and poked one.

"Hey, quit poking me," the mushroom cried.

It was Laser's voice. Excited, she touched the mushroom again. "Laser. It's me. Bianca. I wish you were back to normal."

In an instant, the mushroom changed into Laser. "Boy. How did you do that? I thought I was going to spend the rest of my life two inches tall," he said, admiring the return of his arms and legs.

"I'm not sure. But I'll try it again." She quickly changed the other two mushrooms into Jewel and Lara.

"I dreamed I was a mushroom," said Jewel, spitting out a bit of sand.

"You were a mushroom," said Lara. "It wasn't a dream."

"You weren't playing a violin, were you?" Bianca asked Lara.

"As a mushroom, I think it would be difficult. But I was humming my favorite tune," she replied.

"I guess I must have heard it," said Bianca running her fingers through her hair. It was no longer a tangled mess, as if last night's journey had blown out all the knots.

"I'm confused," said Jewel. "Things have gotten very strange."

"The Wood Nymphs told me they got 'shroom' happy and everyone who was fighting got changed into mushrooms."

"And we were getting the best of them. You should have seen Lara. She actually rode one of the cycles and raced circles around them," said Laser, who rarely complimented girls.

"Where did you learn to ride a motorcycle?" Bianca asked Lara.

"I've played with wrecked ones left behind by Vandals in the valley. They're not hard to start. As the Vandals were leaving the inn, I got on one and started it," said Lara.

"This big burly guy started running toward her, yelling at the top of his lungs, but Lara took off before he could reach her," said Laser.

"I hid in a maple tree and threw rocks at them as part of our ambush," said Jewel.

"You planned it all out?" asked Bianca.

"Of course!" said Laser. "Lara got some Vandals to chase her around the clearing and then into the woods. That's where Jewel and I started pelting them with rocks."

"We were getting the better of them when my cycle overturned on a half-buried log. I jumped off but the Vandals had me surrounded."

Laser began, "Jewel and I picked up these large sticks and raced over to Lara..."

"Then the oddest thing happened," interrupted Jewel. "I could swear that the trees started moving around us. And then everything became a blur."

"It was like they came alive," said Laser.

"The Vandals were just about to grab me when this mist settled over us. It came out of nowhere!" said Lara.

"And now we're here!" said Laser.

Bianca patted him on the back, "Laser, thanks for throwing that tray into the inn. It gave me a chance to escape."

"Hey, I'm ...sorry for causing trouble in the first place," Laser said, blushing a little.

Bianca couldn't recall when Laser had last said he was sorry – for anything. The forest must have a good effect on him, she thought.

"What do we do now?" Jewel asked, wringing her hands. "I'm hungry." She looked around nervously. "Where are we, anyway?"

Before Bianca could reply, a large dark shadow engulfed them.

Laser shouted, "Run! It's a monster!"

Jewel screamed. Lara hugged her. Bianca froze, looking up in awe.

Chapter 23

Over the Tygans

A monstrous, brilliant white stallion, with a shaggy mane and massive wings, soared directly toward Bianca and her friends. With powerful and steady flaps of its wings, the horse landed, its hooves gently touching the ground.

"Watch out, Bianca!" yelled Jewel.

Laser turned to stare at the winged beast.

Bianca felt no fear. She didn't know why; but things had become so unreal and so unexpected, there wasn't time to be afraid.

"I've come with a message from the nymphs." The horse didn't actually speak. Bianca was surprised to hear its voice in her mind, since the Ruby Ring was back in its pouch.

The stallion replied to her thoughts. "You can hear me because the Wood Nymphs trust you. They say your heart is pure in your quest to save Tiara."

"And to find my mother," Bianca added quickly.

"And awaken your father," the horse also added. "You have much to do."

Bianca grimaced, not feeling sure she could meet the challenge. "What kind of message do you have?" she asked.

"The nymphs asked me to fly you over the Tygan Mountains. From there, you shall have to travel on without me. But it will be all down hill until you reach Zurbia."

"You can't take us to Zurbia?" Bianca asked, disappointed.

"Can't fly over there; can't breathe the air because of the smog."

"Smog?" Bianca repeated.

"It's a mist that never leaves Zurbia. But it's made by people, not nature."

"Why do they make it?"

"Because it's too difficult not to make."

Bianca frowned. "I don't understand."

"You will, when you arrive in Zurbia," said the stallion, snorting.

When Jewel heard the horse snort, she cautioned Bianca, "Watch out, he might bite you."

"It's OK," said Bianca. "He's been sent by the Wood Nymphs to fly us over the mountains."

"How do you know?" Jewel asked.

"He told me."

"I didn't hear him say anything," said Jewel, eyeing the horse warily.

"Can the others hear you speak?" Bianca asked the horse.

"No. You're the only one who can hear me."

Bianca explained this to Jewel and Lara.

Laser determined it was safe and rejoined the others. "Did you say he'd fly us over the Tygans?" he asked.

"That's what he said," Bianca replied.

Laser's mouth dropped open.

"Bianca said she can hear his thoughts," Jewel told him.

"I believe her. After spending the night as a mushroom, I'll believe anything," said Laser.

Jewel put her finger up to the side of her head in thought and asked, "Does he have a name?"

Bianca was about to repeat the question when the stallion said, "Call me Eros."

"His name is Eros," said Bianca.

"Do you think this is some kind of trick of the Wizard's?" Jewel asked suspiciously.

"I don't think so. I trust him," Bianca replied.

"Hey, Bianca. What's in his saddle bags?" asked Lara.

Eros then bucked his back feet and jolted the bags off. He moved aside and said, "These are for you."

Bianca opened one; various types of fruit and nuts rolled out of it.

Jewel and Laser rushed to them. "Food, food!" they yelled in unison.

"Look," said Lara, as she pulled out a small knapsack from one of the saddle bags. "Inside is a canteen filled with water. We can also use the knapsack for carrying whatever we don't eat now."

"Tell him thanks for the food and ask him how long it will take us to cross the Tygans," Lara said to Bianca.

Eros replied immediately, "Tell them we must leave soon to arrive before dark."

Bianca told the others. They quickly finished eating and mounted Eros. The stallion spread out wide wings, thick with feathers. The travelers snuggled against the horse's body, comfortably underneath the feathers.

"This is better than a video game," said Laser. Jewel nodded in agreement and yelled back as they rose into the air, "You know, this trip isn't too bad after all."

Higher and higher they climbed into the sky. The giant field of daisies became a small patch of white and yellow dots surrounded by a thick carpet of treetops. The Tygan forest spread before them, all the way to the snow-covered mountain peaks. And with every wing beat, they drew nearer.

Bianca closed her eyes after some time and dreamed of meeting her mother. In her dream, Bianca swooped down from the sky on Eros. Attena reached up to touch Bianca, but there were many strangers standing next to her. They were trying to pull Attena's arms down as she yelled something. Eros just circled high above Attena, never getting any closer.

Bianca cried, "I'm coming, I'm coming," and woke with a start. She glanced around, it had been a dream. The others were fast asleep.

If I don't find Mom, I'm lost, she thought, still shaking from the awful dream. I can't imagine returning to Tiara or staying in Zurbia. What would I do if Mom isn't there? She just didn't know.

Eros flew straight into the setting sun. The mountains were directly under his wings. Cold air rushed by Bianca, but she lay warm and protected under the horse feathers.

"Will we be landing soon?" Bianca asked Eros, trying to forget the dream and wanting to get to Zurbia as soon as possible.

"Yes, very soon. I'm going to land in the Cave of Wishes just on the other side of the mountains."

Eros slowly banked to the left and Bianca felt herself shift slightly. He made a large gentle spiral down to the ground. A few minutes later, with his wings outstretched, Eros glided into the mouth of a mammoth cave.

"I'll spend the night here. You can sleep within my wings. But in the morning you shall have to go on without me."

Bianca thanked Eros and fell asleep again, wondering what this new land would be like.

CHAPTER 24

The Naked Forest

Morning came slowly as the night's deep blackness gradually grayed into a somber day. From the mouth of the cave, Bianca saw an overcast sky. No sunbeams warmed her face. No forest sounds filled the air. There was only an irregular rhythm of water dripping within the cave.

She lay staring at the roof. Overhead, stones the shape of icicles hung from the ceiling. Some were only a few inches long, others several feet. Droplets fell from their tips into pools below them. The cave echoed with their tiny but clear plunking sounds.

"They're called stalactites," said Lara, nodding to stones overhead. "I read about them in the books your grandfather gave me. If you look at the floor of the cave you'll find stalagmites. They're shaped like cones."

Since Eros had slept with his legs folded under his body, Bianca was able to slide down his side to the floor of the cave. "You're right! They are all around here. Hey, this water is warm," Bianca said when she stuck her hand in one of the pools.

"They must be hot springs," said Lara.

Their talking caused Laser and Jewel to stir. "Where are we? This place has a leaky roof," said Jewel, staring up as water dripped down on her.

"It's a giant cave with hot springs," said Lara.

Jewel slid down Eros and joined Bianca. She peered into a nearby pond suspiciously. "Anything in the water? I mean anything alive? Like snakes?"

Just then, Eros snorted. Lara and Laser, who were still on his back, hurriedly slid off him.

Eros stood up. He towered over them like an ivory sculpture. Bianca heard his thoughts.

"I must leave now. Head down the slope. Before the end of the day you, should reach a stream. That stream flows into the River Styx, beyond which lies Zurbia," he told her.

Eros then stepped to the edge of the cave. He spread his wings, which almost stretched from one side of the cave wall to the other. Stamping his right front hoof, the great stallion neighed loudly.

Bianca heard his thoughts once more. "If you need me to fly you back to Tiara, return to this cave."

"How will you know when I get back here?" Bianca asked.

"Use your Ruby Ring," he replied and rose into the sky. The stallion circled once over the Cave of Wishes and then faded into the clouds. They waved good-bye in solemn silence.

No one spoke for awhile as they thought about what lay ahead. Finally, Laser spoke up, "Well, what do we do now?"

They all looked at Bianca, as if waiting for her instructions. She felt awkward being a leader but would do her best and told them Eros's directions.

"Where is Zurbia?" asked Jewel, placing her hand over her eyebrows, as if it would help her see farther.

Before them lay a naked forest of sickly evergreens with barren, twisted branches. Coarse brown grass and skimpy bushes replaced the lush giant ferns found on Tiara's side of the mountains.

But, Zurbia was nowhere to be seen. A few large crows flying overhead were the only signs of life.

"I can understand now why few of our people come here," said Lara. "It looks pretty bleak."

In a short time, they were marching single file out of the cave and down the mountain. Lara went first, followed by Laser, while Bianca kept Jewel company at the back of the line.

The slope was gradual enough to walk down without fear of sliding, and the travelers didn't have to jump over any crevices. Nevertheless, it was a long, strenuous trek.

"I've never walked this far in my life," said Laser. Too exhausted to talk, Jewel nodded in agreement. Even Lara, who was the strongest of them, dragged her feet.

After many hours of walking, a fine layer of dust coated their clothes, hair, ears and at times it seemed, even their tongues. For lunch they sat down on the hard, dry ground to eat the rest of the fruit and nuts. The canteen's water provided welcome but limited relief to their parched throats.

"How long do you think we've been walking?" asked Jewel.

Lara looked up at the overcast sky and shrugged. "Can't tell how far the sun has moved since we began. We'll have to take more breaks so we don't wear ourselves out."

"I'm already worn out," Jewel said in a dry, scratchy voice.

They trudged on for the rest of the day. The bright grayness of the afternoon gave way to successively duller shades as evening approached. To save energy and to keep their mouths moist, no one spoke. Their strides shortened until their feet merely shuffled along.

Bianca encouraged Jewel onward. "The stream should be pretty close," she reassured her, not actually having any idea how far off it was. But she had to keep Jewel moving, out of fear that her friend might collapse from exhaustion.

Tears silently rolled down Jewel's cheeks. If I was a true friend, I should have encouraged her to stay at Mrs. Arbor's, Bianca thought. Now I've gotten her in this mess.

The evening's somber gray light slowly grew ever darker. Doubts about the entire journey swept over Bianca. Would they ever find the stream? Even then, what would they eat? How foolish to have led her friends on this crazy journey. Would they now all die on this barren mountain side?

Suddenly, Lara raised her right arm, and halted their march, then swung around to face the other three.

Bianca studied her friends' tired faces and hoped that Lara had spotted the stream ahead. It would quench their thirst and offer a place to spend the night.

"We have a guest," said Lara with despair. She slowly turned and pointed to a figure about a fifty yards away. It was the Wizard.

CHAPTER 25

Finding Zen

The Wizard faced the horizon, his back turned to them, arms raised slightly to his sides. The long sleeves of his white robe flowed gracefully down, just past his waist. Determination overcame exhaustion as Bianca's doubts vanished. She would get to the Kingdom of Zurbia. He's just a phony and I'm not going to be bullied by him, she thought.

Bianca whispered to Lara, "Let's continue walking." The Wizard's presence revived their spirits. With new-found energy and determination, they marched down the slope. When they were twenty feet away from him, he turned to face them.

Bianca stopped and stared in disbelief. The long white robe, even the white hair and beard were like Neechie's, but that was all. This person was a stranger.

"My name is Zen," he said. "Who are you? And where in the world did you come from?"

Before Bianca could find her voice, Jewel pleaded softly, "Please. Sir, do you have any water?" Her slight body trembled as she spoke.

A warm, charming smile greeted her. "Yes, of course. A stream is only a hundred feet away. There's plenty of water for all of you." Bianca would have shouted with joy, but she barely had enough energy to stand. Along with the others, she smiled and whispered, "Thanks."

"You look like you've been walking a very long time. Come quench your thirst and rest in my cabin." Zen pointed to a rustic dwelling of logs and huge stones, partially hidden by spruces.

They accepted his invitation and followed him. Once inside, they collapsed on a floor of soft, woven grass mats while Zen lit several lanterns. He passed out cups of water to the thirsty travelers and then offered them some vegetable stew that had been simmering on his wood stove. They gratefully devoured it.

Bianca felt stronger after eating and began to wonder why Zen lived alone on the mountain. He seemed friendly and helpful, although his resemblance to Neechie was eerie.

She slid over to a corner of the room while her friends chatted among themselves. Zen had collected the bowls and was now washing them in a tub of water. Discreetly Bianca took out the Ruby Ring and held it tightly.

The Ruby's warmth removed the chill from her hands and made her feel good. She hoped to read Zen's mind and find out more about him.

"Ohm – Ohm – Ohm," the chant rang in her mind. Her eyebrows rose slightly. Why was Zen chanting? Did he suspect that someone was trying to read his mind?

Bianca carefully studied Zen as he cleaned up. His chanting continued. She would question him and hoped to find out, with the help of the Ruby Ring, if he had any evil intentions. With the Ruby in her fist, she walked over and thanked him for the stew.

Zen set the last bowl in the dish drainer. "I don't get guests very often. This is a special occasion," he said and strolled over to a rocking chair.

Bianca sat on the grass mat in front of his chair. "Why are you living up here?" she asked.

Instead of replying, he reached over and picked up a dark wooden pipe. "Do you mind if I smoke? This is my last holdover from Zurbia," he said.

"No. That's OK. I've never been around anyone who smoked a pipe."

"It's not a good habit, but I do allow myself to have this one indulgence."

"Indulgence?" asked Bianca with a quizzical expression.

"Yes, you know. It's the one thing that I spoil myself with. Some people, for instance, indulge themselves by eating or sleeping too much."

"Or losing their temper or crying all the time," offered Bianca.

"Yes. That could be an indulgence, too. Of course, some people place no limit on the number of things that they indulge in," explained Zen.

"Like the Vandals," Bianca said. She was rather proud of herself for coming up with that example.

"Yes. Indeed that is right. Like Vandals."

"Do they ever come up here?" she asked.

"Not yet," he said.

The others became interested in Bianca's conversation with Zen and gathered around his rocking chair.

Jewel pointed to Zen's pipe and said, "Smoking is harmful to your health."

"It's his indulgence," said Bianca, trying to sound older than Jewel.

Zen rocked in his chair, reached into his pocket and took out a box of matches. He lit a match and held it above the bowl of his pipe. He took several puffs on it and blew out perfect little rings.

"Cool!" exclaimed Laser, as the rings floated above their heads.

"How come you live out here?" Bianca persisted in her questioning.

"I used to be a lawyer," Zen replied.

"What's a lawyer?" asked Jewel.

"A lawyer is someone who fights for you," he explained.

"Like a sentry?" asked Lara.

"Not quite. Lawyers fight with words, not fists. When two people disagree about something, they hire a lawyer to fight for them, using words as weapons. The loser then pays the winner money."

"I think the Vandals are more dangerous. When they fight, you end up bleeding, if not dead," said Lara.

"That is true. Vandals are a major problem in Zurbia. Many roam the streets," Zen said.

"Where do they come from?" asked Lara.

"I don't know for sure. Some people say they are the children of lawyers. In any case, I came here to be rid of them and everything else in Zurbia.

"I took work too seriously. I was a lawyer for one of the largest law firms in Zurbia, Aggression Unlimited. We won many fights for our clients."

"I represented, that is, I worked for the car dealers. People complained that Zurbia's air was becoming foul and nasty. Odors and dangerous chemicals, especially lead vapors, were in the air."

"What are lead vapors?" asked Bianca.

"They come from a car's exhaust. And now, after many years, they have formed a fine mist that always hangs over Zurbia. People breathe in the vapors and the lead eventually settles in their brains."

"What happens then?" Lara asked.

Zen gave a sly little smile and said, "Over time, you go crazy."

CHAPTER 26

Delusions of Grandeur

The children glanced at each other and then stared back at Zen. Was he crazy? was the unspoken question on their minds. Laser spoke out next. "How did the lead vapors affect you?"

"I argued that air pollution was the price of becoming modern. You know, to make an omelet you have to break some eggs."

"That makes sense to me," said Laser.

"That sounds crazy to me," Bianca said pointedly to Laser.

"Well, I won the legal arguments, but I lost my soul. I felt dead inside."

"What did you do?" Lara asked.

"I got very depressed and quit my job. For months I would stare lifelessly out of my window, unable to do anything."

"How did you feed yourself?" asked Jewel—food being ever on her mind.

"My brother took care of me until I had a dream. I saw myself living peacefully in the mountains. So the next day, I headed into the hills. The higher I hiked into the mountains, the smaller and smaller Zurbia became. Soon, it was like a speck of sand."

Zen tapped his pipe on the arm of the chair and emptied its ashes into a tray on a small table beside him. Reaching into his shirt pocket, he took out a leather pouch. He pinched some vegetation out of it and stuffed the bowl of his pipe.

"I realized then that I was a speck too," he continued. "I had been so involved in my work, I forgot what life was about.

"So after wandering around the mountains for awhile, I ended up here, a retreat far from a city gone mad with lead poisoning. Up here the air is better. And, after many years of fasting, my body has thrown off those poisons. I can now think clearly," he said wide-eyed.

Zen lit his pipe again and blew several more rings into the air. "The lead in Zurbia's air causes people to develop delusions of grandeur," he said.

"What's a 'delusion of grandeur'?" asked Bianca, her eyebrows knitted.

"That's when you think that what you are doing is the most important thing in the world, for you or anyone else. You lose respect for others."

"Sounds like our Wizard," said Bianca looking down at the floor mat.

"Wizard?" Zen said and laughed.

"Yes. He dresses just like you," said Bianca eyeing her host closer than before.

"I didn't think I dressed as a Wizard," Zen said, still chuckling.

"You were saying 'Ohm' over and over again," said Bianca.

Zen was startled. "Did I? I guess I must have been mumbling it out loud. It's just a simple chant to make me feel peaceful." He then looked long and hard at Bianca.

Bianca read his thoughts: "It's almost as if she could read my mind. She seems so intense and inquisitive."

"But enough talk about me," he said aloud. "I have yet to learn what brought you here."

"We're traveling from Tiara," said Bianca.

"From Tiara! How in the world did you make it over the mountains? Where are your parents? You must be traveling with them or others."

"We came by ourselves. We're on a mission to Zurbia," said Laser.

Bianca shot Laser a dirty look. She didn't want anyone talking about their "mission" until she was sure Zen could be trusted.

"So what are you going to do in Zurbia? Join the Vandals?" Zen asked with a wink.

Laser opened his mouth as if to answer Zen, but closed it abruptly when he saw Bianca glaring at him.

Lara and Jewel waited to see what Bianca would say. Bianca

held the Ruby Ring. So far, Zen's thoughts were the same as his words. He didn't seem to be lying.

There was an awkward period of silence. Zen looked at Bianca and said, "Well, it seems that we're all waiting for you to tell us the purpose of this mission."

Bianca took a deep breath and said, "We're looking for my mother, Attena."

"You're Attena's daughter?"

Bianca couldn't believe what she heard. "You know her?"

"Not directly, I only knew of her through my brother. He passed through here about a year ago." Zen smiled at Bianca. "He was on the same mission as you. He wanted to find Attena."

Bianca and her friends looked puzzled. "What do you mean? Bianca asked.

"The King of Zurbia sent him to Tiara to ask Attena to visit his kingdom. The King knew of your mother's reputation for helping people solve problems."

Bianca studied Zen for a moment. "You're Neechie's brother! That's why you look and dress like him."

"My brother does have a white beard. And I gave him one of my white robes. He was very fond of it. So I guess I do look like him."

Although Bianca didn't hear any thoughts other than what Zen had spoken, she still didn't trust him. How could he be Neechie's brother and still be a good person?

Bianca stood up. An angry scowl crossed her face. She exploded, "Your brother poisoned my father and wants to destroy our kingdom!"

CHAPTER 27

The Wizard's Past

Zen hung his head and spoke softly, "My brother is capable of evil deeds. But he wasn't always that way. When he was much younger, he wanted to make life better for others."

Zen sat up and looked at his guests. "But over time, the lead poisoning affected him. He developed delusions of grandeur; no one had the right answers but him. Because he is a genius, he dazzled people with his knowledge and his magical tricks. But his arrogance became his downfall."

"What happened?" asked Bianca.

Before Zen could reply, Laser blurted out, "Then he does know magic?"

"Please one question at a time," Zen said wearily. He took a moment to collect his thoughts and began again.

"My brother was the adviser to the King of Zurbia. But the King ignored his advice. He was very frustrated when a group of citizens asked the King to invite your mother to Zurbia. They had heard of her wise decisions and also knew that Tiara was being increasingly harassed by Vandals. They figured if she could help Zurbia then Tiara would also benefit because Zurbia would then produce fewer Vandals. My brother then volunteered to carry the message to Tiara in the hope that your Kingdom would better appreciate his talents. He really believed that he could improve your Kingdom."

"And as far as his magic is concerned, I believe it is as real as people want it to be. For instance, he used it to convince some Vandals to take him over the Tygans to Tiara. But they wanted to believe in it because he also promised to make them rich."

"How could he make them rich?" asked Bianca, suspiciously.

"Zurbians need more wood for building and heating their

homes. Their biggest trees were cut down long ago and they never bothered to replant new ones. Acid rain ruined the remaining trees."

Zen gently tapped his pipe on the edge of his chair and lit it again. "My brother dreamed of building a road over the Tygans to cut down trees on the other side. He could become rich selling them to Zurbia."

"Could he actually build a road over the Tygans?" asked Lara.

"It would be almost impossible. Even though my brother is very smart, I don't think even he could do it. The mountains are too high. The only pass through them is very narrow and closed for half the year because of snow and mud slides."

Bianca recalled the Vandals talking at the Last Inn about Neechie's plan to build the road. "Neechie was excited about some information that Attena had sent with one of her messengers. Do you know what it could have been?" she asked.

"No, I don't," Zen replied. He casually blew some "O's" into the air.

Bianca watched them swirl around until they melted into the air and said, "We received a message saying that my Mom died in a landslide, traveling through the mountains."

Zen didn't say anything and the ruby, still in Bianca's grip, didn't relay any of his thoughts.

"I think she's still alive in Zurbia," Bianca declared. "I'm going to bring her back to Tiara."

"Why hasn't she come home before this?" Zen asked casually.

"I'm sure there's a reason, a very good reason," Bianca answered firmly. But then added softly, "I just don't know what it is." Her throat swelled slightly and her eyes became teary. She didn't want to appear weak in front of him and fought back the anger and frustration in not knowing why her mother had not returned.

"I'm sure there is a good reason why she hasn't returned,"

Zen said gently, appearing to sense her feeling of confusion and loss. He looked very old, even ancient, in the dim glow of the lanterns.

"Perhaps Attena didn't return because she has been affected by lead poisoning. It changes the behavior of even the best and smartest people in strange ways," he suggested.

Bianca nodded slowly, pondering that awful possibility.

"And your father?" Zen asked hesitantly. "You say my brother poisoned him?"

"Yes, he is in a deep sleep. He can't be awakened."

Zen looked startled. "Asleep?"

"Yes." Bianca did not look at Zen. She stared off into the darkness of the room around her. She felt alone. Would she ever get her parents back?

"I may be able to help you. I gave my brother two gifts. One was the robe. The other was a special herb."

Bianca looked back at him curiously.

"My brother had difficulty falling asleep. So I gave him a special herb to help him sleep. I warned him that he should use only a pinch of it. If he took too much he could fall into a deep sleep and never wake."

Bianca's eyes grew large. "You supplied the poison!" she shouted.

"I gave it to him as a medicine, not a poison. I'm sorry." Zen slouched in his chair and rested his head in his hands.

"Is there an antidote to end the sleeping sickness?" asked Lara.

"I got the herb from a hermit who had lived alone in the mountains. He told me that the Mir flower was the only antidote."

"Where can we find it?" Bianca asked anxiously.

"Unfortunately, pollution killed it off many years ago," Zen sadly replied.

"But it might be on our side of the mountains where there isn't pollution, right?" she asked hopefully.

"It's possible," Zen said. He then straightened up in his chair and set his pipe down on the end table. "I'm sorry my brother caused you pain. I had hoped his absence from Zurbia would have changed him for the better. But I guess a year is not long enough to throw off the effects of lead poisoning."

He rose from his chair and advised his travelers, "Morning will come soon enough and you'll have to be on your way. It's time for bed."

He brought out some blankets for his guests and spread them out on the grass mats. The wood stove kept the cabin comfortably warm and soon they were all asleep.

When they awoke the next morning, Zen was gone.

CHAPTER 28

The River Styx

L ara rose first and scouted outside the cabin. She returned to report that there was no sign of Zen.
Laser and Jewel got up next. Jewel didn't look well. "I'm getting a cold. I need some medicine," she said wiping her nose with her sleeve.

"Great, Sis, I knew you should have stayed behind!"

"Laser, back off. It's just a cold," said Lara. She began searching the cabin's shelves. "Maybe Zen has some kind of medicine you could use."

Not finding anything, she sat down at the kitchen table and then cried out, "Hey Bianca. Here's a note from Zen!"

Bianca got up, rushed over and began reading it aloud:

> *Dear Bianca and friends,*
>
> *Sorry to not see you off, but I meditate alone each morning. There's some oatmeal in the pot for your breakfast. I've also left some apples and muffins for you to take with you.*
>
> *After you've eaten, follow the stream downhill until it runs into a large river. It is the River Styx. I have a row boat hidden among the reeds where the stream enters the river. Although I've never taken it all the way, I believe the River Styx leads to Zurbia. You're welcome to take the boat there.*
>
> *May your mission be a success.*
>
> *Zen*

"We should eat and head out as soon as possible," proposed Lara. "Who knows how far we'll have to walk downstream before reaching the boat?"

Bianca and the rest agreed. They ate breakfast, cleaned up, packed their knapsack and left a thank-you note for Zen.

"Do you think we'll ever see Zen again? He seemed like such a nice man. I wish the Wizard was like his brother," Jewel said as she closed the cabin door behind them.

They followed the stream for a few hours before reaching the River Styx. Bianca was lost in her thoughts about Zen; he seemed so different from Neechie, and yet they were brothers, so they must have something in common. What was it?

She snapped out of her daydreaming when Lara shouted, "I've found the boat. It's in these reeds, just like Zen said, where the stream enters the river." Lara stood in the marsh, past her knees in a mixture of the oozing mud and water.

The others wadded into the marsh to help Lara. "Yuk!" said Jewel, sinking up to her thighs in the silty bottom. "I can barely move in this pudding," she said, pressing her shoulder against the boat.

After vigorously rocking the boat back and forth, they freed it from the mud and shoved into the river.

Once on board, Bianca and Laser each took an oar and started rowing. A strong current caught the boat and it easily drifted downstream.

They leisurely floated along, eating their fill of muffins and apples. Between huge billowing clouds, the sun occasionally shined down upon them. A steady but warm breeze made it a lovely day to reflect on their journey and to daydream about what might lie ahead of them.

The sun had passed the midday mark when Lara noticed the current had picked up. "We seem to be drifting faster," she said, pointing to the river bank. "Let's keep our eyes open for rocks. There could be rapids ahead."

The current grew stronger throughout the afternoon. The broad, grassy river banks gradually shrank away. The boat was soon sweeping through a canyon, between tall rocky cliffs.

"There's no place to land," said Lara, sounding worried.

"That means we can't stop," Jewel said, surveying the increasingly choppy waters.

Bianca and Laser muscled their oars to keep the boat from crashing onto the boulders. Lara straddled the boat between them, leaning first one way then the other to steady the craft. Jewel sat in the bow guiding them.

After they shot through the canyon, the river became wider but the current remained strong. They spoke little and kept watch for boulders and whirlpools.

"Do you think we've gone past the roughest part?" asked Jewel, whose face seemed almost solid red with freckles.

Lara was about to answer, but hesitated. "Do you hear a roaring noise?" she asked anxiously.

Jewel shrugged her shoulders and looked at Bianca, as if to ask, "Do you hear anything?" In a few moments however, the roar was heard by all. She yelled over to Bianca, "What is it?"

Before Bianca could answer, the boat rounded a bend. The river just seemed to disappear ahead of them. Desperately they tried to row toward shore.

Lara yelled, "Grab onto the side of the boat!" Jewel screamed and a moment later all that could be heard was the deafening roar of a waterfall.

CHAPTER 29

Using the Ruby

B ianca felt herself being lifted out of her seat as the boat plunged over the edge of the waterfall. Her hands gripped the side of the boat, but they were wrenched away by a torrent of rushing water. Desperately gulping for air, she closed her eyes and tumbled through space.

The sky and waterfall became one, until she hit the river. Water pounded down on her, churning the river and pulling Bianca under.

She frantically kicked her legs and stretched her arms up. Finally, she broke through to the surface and gasped for air.

Although light-headed, she looked about for her friends, particularly Jewel. Lara and Laser were both strong swimmers but Jewel wasn't.

The Ruby Ring could help me find her, Bianca thought. She carefully took it out of the pouch, knowing that one fumbling move would mean losing it forever.

As she grasped the ring, a cry shot through her head: "*Help me. I'm drowning.*" It was Jewel.

Bianca eyes raced across the surface of the river, there was no sign of her. She concentrated and thought, "*Jewel! please hear me. Where are you? I can't see you*".

There was nothing but silence. She tried again, squeezing her eyes and picturing Jewel in her mind. Then like a whisper, she heard Jewel.

"*I'm caught on a log under the falls. I can't keep treading water much longer*".

Bianca spotted a log and swam toward the fall. "*Hang on, I'm coming to help you*", she thought. But there was no response. She decided to keep a grip on the ruby in case she lost sight of Jewel.

The falling water fanned out before her, creating a heavy mist. Through it she saw Jewel's arm draped over the top of the log. Bianca took a deep breath and dove under it to reach Jewel. She resurfaced next to her friend, under the down pouring falls.

Jewel was barely able to speak. Her shirt had caught onto a branch and had kept her afloat.

Bianca unsnagged her shirt but couldn't lift Jewel over the log. She would have to take her back under it to more open water. From there, Jewel could be safely pulled to shore.

The Ruby Ring was still in her hand – she needed to put it away, but the pounding water made it impossible to retrieve her pouch or to even open her fist without possibly dropping the ruby.

She placed one arm around Jewel, leaving the other free to paddle. Bianca breathed in deeply several times. Down they went.

Her leg muscles pumped hard, fighting to keep them from being dragged under by the current. With her lungs aching and her head dizzy from lack of oxygen, she finally bobbed up, gasping for air. Jewel had passed out but Bianca managed to keep her head above the water.

Then it happened, in a twitch of exhaustion her grip around the Ruby Ring slackened. It slipped between her fingers. Bianca watched the dazzling stone sink in the clear water. She quickly stabbed at it. But it was in vain as the Ruby grew fainter and became a mere speck lost in the deep waters below.

Her heart sank with the realization that she had lost the Ruby Ring of Tiara – forever.

Although in shock, Bianca managed to pull Jewel to shore. They lay exhausted on a sandy beach as the water lapped at their feet. Blurry eyed, she saw Lara running toward them. "Bianca, you saved Jewel!"

Lara quickly revived Jewel. After coughing up some water, she opened her dazed eyes.

Bianca slumped next to Jewel, too weak to speak, just gazing up at the waterfall. We must have fallen twenty feet, she thought.

A drenched Laser stood nearby. His gadget belt still hung

around his waist. "Hey, I started a fire to dry us out," he called out to the others. "Luckily I had another lighter in my gadget belt. And it stayed dry," he said proudly.

Lara ran off to collect more firewood. Laser tended the fire, placing small twigs on top of the little flames. As the fire grew, he added branches. Soon he had a blaze going.

Bianca and Jewel huddled together at the edge of it. Bianca's back was cold and clammy, while her face felt toasted by the flames. Still, the heat comforted her.

It was dusk before Jewel spoke for the first time. "Bianca, I thought I was going to drown for sure. Then I heard your voice. The next thing I remember was being on shore."

"I'm glad you're OK. For awhile there, I thought we'd both drown." Bianca wrapped her arm around Jewel.

Trembling, Jewel said, "Maybe I shouldn't have come along. I was supposed to be our lookout and I didn't even see the waterfall. And then I go and almost drown us!"

"None of us saw the waterfall in time, so forget it. And, I'm glad you came," Bianca reassured her.

"Hey," Laser interrupted them. "I'm getting hungry. Is there anything to eat?"

"Our knapsack made it to shore," Lara said. "I can fill it with wild berries I found while looking for firewood. That will at least feed us for now."

"I feel rested," said Bianca. "I'll help you." With a slight wobble, Bianca got up and slowly followed her friend.

When they had passed out of sight from the others, Bianca stopped Lara. At first she couldn't speak. Only tears came to her eyes.

"What's wrong?" asked Lara.

"I've lost the Ruby Ring. It's at the bottom of the river." Bianca sat down and drew her knees to her chin. Lara knelt beside her.

"I guess you used it to find Jewel. But it's gone now. We just have to continue on," she said calmly.

"That's easy for <u>you</u> to say. <u>I'm</u> the one who lost it!" cried Bianca, shivering. She buried her face in her crossed arms. Lara gently rested her arm around Bianca's narrow shoulders.

"I can't believe I lost the Ruby Ring," sobbed Bianca, unable to hold back her grief.

"You saved your best friend's life with it. Jewel would have drowned. It was worth the trade: a human life for a stone," Lara comforted her.

"I know. I'd do anything to save Jewel or you, or Laser. But it wasn't just a stone. It really was magic. Real magic! Not trickery! You don't understand. It was the most amazing thing. You could actually listen to people's thoughts. You could get inside of their minds."

"Still, no gem, no matter how magical, is ever worth as much as a human life," Lara said.

"But I needed it to find Mom and get us back to Tiara," Bianca insisted.

"We're almost there. We will find Attena. And we'll make it back to Tiara. Your mission is almost over." Lara was just as insistent.

"How do you know?" Bianca asked.

"I just know."

Bianca wanted to be like Lara, strong and confident. She heaved a sigh and got up. "Please don't say anymore." Wiping the back of her hand across her face, she added, "I don't want Laser to know I've been crying." She was in no mood for his teasing.

"He won't know. It's getting dark anyway," Lara said.

"Please keep quiet about this. I have to tell Mom before anybody else," said Bianca.

"I won't tell a soul," Lara promised, as they walked back.

Quietly, they all huddled around the campfire, eating berries. The flames danced about and the embers glowed bright red and orange. Slowly Bianca's eyelids closed.

She dreamed of the waterfall and how it grew ever larger

and louder, until it shook the ground. She awoke with a start.

In the gray dawn, she could see Lara and Laser huddled nearby, peering over a fallen tree. Laser turned to see that she was awake. He called across to her in a hushed voice, "Vandals!"

CHAPTER 30

Getting Hip

"What's going on?" asked Jewel, rubbing the sleep out of her eyes.

"Shush," cautioned Bianca. "Vandals are nearby." She pointed toward the bushes where Lara and Laser were kneeling. Jewel squeezed Bianca's arm.

"It's OK. They haven't seen us. Let's take a look," said Bianca.

"Ah ...you go ahead. I'll stay here," Jewel said apprehensively.

Bianca tiptoed over to Lara and peered over a log.

"They just drove up on their cycles," whispered Lara. "This underbrush protected us from being discovered."

"They came close enough to wake me up," Bianca whispered back.

"They have a captive," said Lara, referring to a person gagged and sitting on the ground. He was a young man, wearing a tweed sports coat and brown-framed glasses. His hands were bound behind him. The Vandals took turns taunting him.

"You think you're so smart because you're a librarian, do you?" said a fat Vandal whose blubbery belly bulged below his T-shirt. He jabbed a book into the librarian's ribs and then ripped it in half.

"Well, your smarts aren't going to help you out now. We're sick and tired of your kind, always telling others what is right and wrong. As if all the answers were in books," the fat one went on. Meanwhile, the other three Vandals tossed books into a pile.

The librarian protested, violently shaking his brown, shaggy head of hair.

Another Vandal, stocky and built like a bull, held a can of gasoline and began sprinkling its contents over the pile of books. He stepped back and then threw a lit match. A bonfire erupted with a great whishing noise. Long thin flames licked toward the sky. The Vandals howled and doubled over with laughter.

Afterward, they stood silently watching the flames, as if hypnotized. Then Jewel sneezed.

The stocky Vandal glanced in their direction. Bianca and the others ducked behind the log. "Did you hear someone sneeze?" asked one of the Vandals.

Jewel sneezed again. "I'm sorry. It won't happen again," she called out in a hushed voice to her friends.

"I definitely heard it this time," said the same Vandal.

"I thought I heard a voice too," said another. Twigs and dried branches started cracking under heavy boots.

"They're heading this way," Laser said, anxiously.

Bianca looked back to warn Jewel. But she was gone.

"Hey, creeps, over here!" Jewel shouted from a clump of bushes far off to the side of the log.

"Grab her!" shouted a Vandal. Bianca heard them race away.

"Now's our chance," Lara said, peering over the log. "I'll grab one of their cycles and get Jewel. The two of you untie the librarian."

Bianca picked up a tree branch to act as a club and leaped over the log with Laser. Whipping out a small pocket knife, Laser cut the cords binding the librarian's hands and feet.

"Thanks, whoever you are," said the librarian, untying his gag.

"Let's get out of here before they come back," Bianca yelled and grabbed his hand to lead him back to their campsite.

"Not that way," the librarian said as he tugged Bianca back. "Let's ride," he said, running toward a cycle. He pointed to its sidecar. "The two of you hop in."

"Shouldn't we mess these up so they can't follow us," suggested Bianca, pointing to two other bikes.

"Good idea," said the librarian, pulling some wires from their motors. "And for good measure puncture their tires as well," he ordered Laser.

"No problem," said Laser, stabbing his pocket knife into them.

Bianca jumped into the small side car and then looked up at

Laser. "You can't possibly fit in here too."

Laser's mouth opened, about to say something, when the librarian yelled, "Just jump on the seat behind me."

Still standing in the side car, Bianca could see Lara riding off on a cycle with two Vandals running after her. Suddenly Bianca was jerked down into her seat as they roared off - after the Vandals!

CHAPTER 31

Zurbian Vista

The two Vandals chasing Lara suddenly turned around to look at the cycle bearing down on them. They immediately charged the bike on foot, shouting and waving their arms. The librarian bee lined his cycle toward the nearest Vandal.

A few feet before colliding, the Vandal lost his nerve and dove to the side of the oncoming cycle. He stumbled, fell over and hit his head on a rock.

The second Vandal kept coming, swinging a long thin, bicycle chain above his head. The whirling chain cut the air like a fan blade. Laser raised his arm to protect his face. The Vandal lunged toward the cycle, but the librarian swerved away.

Bianca realized she still held the tree branch and heaved it toward the Vandal's head. It hit him square in the forehead. He grunted and then toppled backward, releasing the bike chain. It whizzed over their heads and harmlessly sailed past.

Moments later they were bearing down on the last two Vandals, who had been chasing Jewel. But the undergrowth grew thicker and grabbed at the wheel spokes, slowing their pursuit.

"We'll never catch them," Laser yelled, disappointed. as they watched the Vandals disappear into the forest.

The librarian halted the cycle. "We can't go much farther in this stuff," he said.

"But what about Lara and Jewel?" Bianca asked.

The librarian turned from side to side in his seat surveying the landscape.

"Cheer up, I see them now," said the librarian, wheeling his cycle half around toward them. Bianca and Laser yelled Lara's name until she heard them and put on her brakes.

"They never even laid a hand on us," gloated Jewel, sitting behind Lara.

Lara laughed. "I got to Jewel before the Vandals and then just stomped on the gas. Did you see where they went?" she asked.

"We took care of two of them, but the rest ran into the underbrush," Laser said. Turning to Jewel, he added, "You almost got us killed! With your stupid sneezing!"

"We weren't in that much danger, Laser. They were pretty out-of-shape," said Lara.

"I thought they might have heard my sneezing", Jewel began to explain, "so I knew I had to do something. I tried to get them away from their cycles so Lara could grab one of them, like she did at the Last Inn."

"You should have told us what you were planning," Laser said, still lecturing her.

"I think things worked out well," the librarian said cheerfully. "Thanks for freeing me. My name's Hip."

"It was nothing. We do this all the time," joked Laser.

"That smart-mouth is my brother Laser. I'm Jewel, this here is Lara, and Bianca is sitting in your sidecar," said Jewel.

"Glad to meet you," said Lara. "Why did they tie you up and burn those books?" she asked.

"I was doing a mobile library trip. You know, going from neighborhood to neighborhood in Zurbia setting up a little table, lending out books and signing up membership in the library. This is my cycle and the sidecar you're sitting in was filled with books."

"Vandals hate books because they fear knowledge. So when they saw what I was doing, they ran me off the road and took me up here. They wanted to make sure that I didn't ever return to their neighborhood." Hip ran his finger across his throat for emphasis.

"We must be close to Zurbia," said Bianca excitedly. "That's where we're headed."

"We're about an hour away. But let's not stay here talking. Other Vandals may be around and those who got away could come back. I know of an isolated grassy knoll, off of the road, where we can rest and talk."

"Can we see the city from there?" asked Laser.

"Do we have anything to eat? I'm starving," Jewel blurted.

"Yes, we can see the city from there. And I think we may have some food as well," Hip said and opened a small compartment on the back of the sidecar. He took out a hunk of cheese and some rolls. "It isn't much, but it should keep you going until we reach the city."

"OK, we're off to Zurbia!" shouted Bianca.

In a cloud of dust, both cycles took off down the road.

Part Three: SAVING THE FUTURE

CHAPTER 32

Smoggy Bottom

Bianca and her friends reached the viewpoint and stretched out on the grass. Hip passed out the rolls and broke off pieces of cheese for everyone.

The morning mist slowly lifted, revealing a broad plain before them, empty of life: no farms, no cows, not even trees, just scrub brush and brown grass. A black-topped road cut straight across the land, leading to Zurbia. But the city itself was shrouded in a thick yellowish fog.

"That must be smog," ventured Bianca.

"That's what it is. Some days it covers the entire plain," said Hip.

As they sat eating, the sun rose higher in the sky, and Zurbia's yellow veil gradually lifted, revealing the city.

Bianca gazed down on the Wizard's Zurbia. It was huge! The entire Kingdom of Tiara, both town and valley, could be swallowed whole by this metropolis.

But it seemed to be a lifeless world. Unlike Tiara, with its bright yellow, red and blue bricks, Zurbia was a dreary mass of gray, square and rectangular buildings. Those at its center towered much higher than Tiara's palace. Streets cut across the town at right angles, making Zurbia appear like a large waffle iron.

"Awesome," said Laser, taking in the immensity of this strange city.

"What were those columns holding up?" asked Bianca, pointing to the plain below them. Columns of brown bricks were scattered throughout the barren plain.

"Those aren't columns, they used to be chimneys. Long

before I was born, wooden box-like houses covered this entire plain. Each had a fireplace that burned logs, but when the trees became scarce they were no longer used," Hip explained.

"But what happened to the houses?" Jewel asked.

"They've returned to dust," said Hip. "It became too dangerous living in a single house with just your family. If Vandals couldn't break into your home, they set fire to it. Rather than rebuilding, people moved into the city for protection."

"It doesn't look like a friendly place to me," Bianca said, tossing her hair out of her eyes. "And there's no wall to keep the Vandals out," she added.

"They're already inside," explained Hip, his glasses perched halfway down his nose. "The townspeople asked our king to control the Vandals. But instead, he makes laws that stop people from criticizing him. So the Vandals do as they please."

Hip slapped his knee and laughed, "You obviously aren't from Zurbia!" He studied his rescuers carefully for the first time. "You're just kids. Where did you come from?"

"You're not so old yourself," said Lara.

"OK, so I'm just 18, but I'm still older than any of you. Did you cross the Tygan Mountains?" he asked.

"We're from Tiara," Bianca said proudly.

"I've heard Tiara's air is free from smog," Hip said.

Bianca nodded and stared back at the thin yellow mist that hung over the sprawling city.

"So what causes it?" asked Lara.

"It comes from car emissions," he answered.

"Car emissions?'" asked Bianca.

"That's the exhaust and smoke coming out of a car's tailpipe," Hip explained. "You wouldn't know, though. Tiara doesn't have cars, does it?"

"That's right, although we have books that show what cars look like. It's just that a long time ago my grandfather banned them from our Kingdom. He thought cars would be bad for us. So we've gotten by using bicycles and horses," Bianca explained.

"You're not only missing out on smog but also acid rain. And that stuff is strong enough to strip paint off buildings," Hip explained.

"The Wood Nymphs told me about the acid rain," said Bianca.

"Wood Nymphs! You have an active imagination," said Hip as he slid his glasses up to the bridge of his nose.

"You don't need an imagination to believe in Wood Nymphs," said Laser.

"If you spent the night as a mushroom, you'd believe in them, too," added Lara.

Hip shook his head in disbelief. "You are an odd bunch. I still don't understand how you crossed the Tygans?"

"Eros brought us here," said Laser.

"Who is Eros?" asked Hip.

"He's a giant, flying stallion," replied Bianca.

"You are some storyteller. Yet, I have to admit you are here. And you're my friends. So, what do you plan to do in Zurbia?" Hip asked, eyeing them carefully.

"I'm looking for my mother, Attena," said Bianca.

"I've read about Attena. She helped solve some major disputes," Hip said.

Bianca's face lit up. "Have you met her?"

"No," Hip replied.

Bianca sighed. "When was the last time you heard of her?"

"I don't remember. It's been awhile, about half a year ago," he answered.

"That's when we received a note from the King of Zurbia saying she died in a landslide, crossing the Tygans," Bianca said.

"O-oh," Hip said thoughtfully.

"But, I don't believe it," Bianca added defiantly. "I know she's still alive in Zurbia."

"What kind of disputes did she settle?" asked Lara, encouraging Hip to talk more about Attena.

"Dangerous chemicals, especially lead vapors from car emissions, pollute our air. Some people didn't want any more cars sold. Of course, the car dealers objected. So Attena got them to compromise."

"What did they agree to?" asked Bianca.

"She had the car dealers give away one bicycle with every car sold. The car dealers were happy because they sold more cars. But eventually, under Attena's plan more people would be pedaling bikes than driving cars, so there would be less pollution in the future."

"Do you think you could help me find her?" Bianca asked.

"Yes, of course," Hip replied.

"How long would it take? Could we find her this afternoon?" she asked eagerly.

Hip scratched his head and glanced at his watch. "It's possible. We could reach Zurbia in an hour or so. I live in an apartment building on this side of town. You can clean up at my place if you'd like. I can round up some fresh clothes for you as well," he said, eyeing their ragged, dusty appearance.

"While you change I'll check our 'Information Please System' at the library. I'm sure they'll have Attena's ..." Hip hesitated. Bianca wondered if he doubted that Attena was still alive. Hip looked at her and smiled. "They'll have her work address."

"Well, let's go," said Bianca, her skin tingled in anticipation of finally seeing her mother.

They mounted their motorcycles and drove down a windy road to the plain and on to the veiled city of Zurbia, home of the Vandals.

CHAPTER 33

A Different World

Like giant dead beetles, abandoned cars littered the roadside outside Zurbia. Scrawny leafless weeds sprouted around their rusted frames and in some cases, where their floors had wasted away, the weeds grew inside.

"Why don't they fix them?" Bianca asked Hip.

"No need to. There's always new ones you can buy."

"They should just fix the old ones," Bianca asserted.

"If we did that, we wouldn't make new ones. And that would put people out of work," said Hip.

"That would be great," said Laser. "Then they could play."

"You can't just play. Everyone has to work. I'm sure even in Tiara, people have to work."

Bianca thought about that for awhile. It was true, people did work in Tiara. But somehow it was different. They made things like bricks for building or grew food that people ate. Things weren't made to be thrown away.

As they drew closer to the city, it appeared that the plain halted abruptly in front of what looked to be a row of monstrous teeth. Soon she could see that they were wooden, rectangular buildings rising above the dry, cracked earth. Each was as tall as Tiara's palace.

Their road aimed for a gap between two of the giant teeth. A huge iron sign arched between them, framing the gap. It read: "Home of the Future." It was an uncaring future, Bianca thought. The buildings were like the cars, ignored and falling apart, with broken windows and peeling paint.

A feeling of dread settled over Bianca when she passed under the sign and into the mouth of the monster. Would this be Tiara's future? she wondered.

It seemed that all of Zurbia consisted of tall, wooden buildings with row upon row of little windows. Heads poked out of them to watch the cycles pass. They wore expressions as bleak and vacant as the plain outside the city.

Someone yelled from a window, but Bianca couldn't hear what was said. A beer bottle flew through the air and shattered on the side of the road, spraying glass just behind them.

Broken bottles carpeted the sidewalks. Parked cars, colors dulled, bumpers and fenders dented, and headlights rusted outlined the road. There wasn't a tree in sight. But slowly the city came alive; people scurried along narrow sidewalks next to the gloomy apartment buildings.

Children in tattered clothing darted into the street, yelling as the travelers rode by. Scabs and sores covered their thin arms and faces. Some raised their cupped hands, begging for handouts.

More cars appeared on the road, and then several motorcycles. Bianca flinched. Vandals! But the motorcycles behaved no differently than the cars and trucks that soon choked the road. They all drove wildly, racing to fill whatever open space, no matter how small, lay ahead of them.

Like giant beetles, cars swarmed over the road, honking their horns, screeching to a halt and even crashing into each other. Drivers would jump out of the cars shouting, their fists swinging wildly in the air.

Amid this chaos, people dodged vehicles trying to cross the street. Mothers dragged screaming children behind them as they dashed from one side of the road to the other. Old people hobbled along, while people in cars, unaware or unconcerned, zoomed by just missing them by inches.

Although the noise was deafening, the foul odors were worse. This town smells worse than Dad's socks, thought Bianca.

So many vehicles crowded onto the street that Bianca's cycle had to slow to crawl. Suddenly Hip took a sharp right turn and darted into an alley behind a building. A large garage door rolled up and they drove inside.

Small overhead lights revealed cobwebs hanging from the

ceiling of a large underground parking garage. Shallow black pools of motor oil covered a grungy concrete floor.

Hip wheeled his cycle into a corner and motioned to Lara to park beside him. A heavy odor of mildew filled the air.

"It really smells bad in here," remarked Jewel.

"It's not the best of parking garages but it's about average," said Hip, leading them up some dimly lit stairs to his home.

The hallway outside his apartment had a worn-down, red shag carpet. Apartment doors with large, black numbers lined each side of the narrow hallway. Bare light bulbs hung from the ceiling.

The place gave Bianca the creeps. For the first time she had some doubts about Hip. Could someone really good live in such a dismal place? Maybe all the people in Zurbia were crazy or Vandals.

Hip rapped twice on door number 120. It squeaked open without Bianca seeing anyone inside. "After you," Hip said, waving in his new-found friends.

CHAPTER 34

The Feast of Freedom

Wispy, curling ribbons of burning incense drifted toward the open door, burning Bianca's eyes as she stepped into the apartment. She rubbed them and tried to focus. Before her was a room that seemed to be both kitchen and living room. Dirty dishes and glasses were piled high on a large table, clothes were draped over some chairs and scattered about the floor, and fallen stacks of books and magazines fanned out of every corner. It looks even worse than my bedroom, thought Bianca.

Suddenly, Bianca's wrist was gripped by a sharp bony hand. Startled, she wrenched her arm away.

"What have you brought back this time?" asked a throaty voice, sounding more surprised than angry.

Bianca stared eye-to-eye into an old woman's wrinkled face. With the striking exception of a pair of bright red lips and black-framed glasses, a thick coating of face powder gave her a ghostly appearance.

"These are visitors from another planet," said Hip, grinning.

"We are not from another planet," Jewel sharply corrected him. She stepped to the other side of Bianca, putting some distance between this strange woman and herself.

"Well you look like you dragged yourself around this planet," said the woman, peering over her glasses.

"I guess we are rather dirty," said Bianca, looking down at her dusty clothes.

"This is my mom, Garbo. She's the best mom in the world, but sometimes she gets a little cranky," said Hip, teasing.

With the incense smoke swirling around them, Jewel and Laser began coughing.

"Let's open a window, Mom, and air out this place. Your incense is pretty strong," said Hip, closing the door behind him.

He then walked to the other side of the room and opened a window.

"It's too polluted out there," explained Garbo to Bianca. "So I keep the windows closed and burn incense."

Bianca politely nodded while Laser and Jewel joined Hip at the window for some air.

"I'll get you some towels so you can shower and clean up," said Garbo, as she rummaged through a large pile of towels stuffed into a closet.

While her visitors took showers, Garbo rifled through a couple of old trunks, looking for clothes to offer them. "I never throw anything away," she explained, unfolding two pleated skirts, one red, the other navy blue, and two white blouses.

Bianca and Jewel had never seen pleated skirts, but they were thankful for the clean, fresh clothing.

Garbo also unearthed a couple of jeans from Hip's younger years for Lara and Laser. They weren't the perfect fit for either of them, but they, too, were clean.

During a lunch of macaroni and cheese, Bianca and the others told of their journey from Tiara.

"Thank you for saving Hip. The Vandals grow bolder every day. It's the lead in the air. It makes people go crazy; they lose any sense of order," said Garbo.

Bianca glanced around and wondered if there was a link between disorderly rooms and lead poisoning.

"Mom was asked to help make Zurbia a better place," said Bianca. "But, we need her in Tiara, or it'll become another Zurbia."

"You just need greed for that," said Hip. Then he suddenly jumped from his seat. "I just remembered. Tonight begins the Feast of Freedom!"

"It's more like the Feast of Fear," said Garbo sullenly.

"What do you mean? Is it a holiday?" asked Lara.

"Long ago it started off as a celebration of being free from tyranny," said Hip.

"Tyranny?" asked Jewel.

"It's when someone makes all the rules and everybody has to obey them," Hip replied.

"But things started to go wrong with the celebration," said Garbo, in her husky voice. "After awhile it became a holiday for breaking all rules."

"It's true, this evening Vandals will be running wild throughout Zurbia," Hip continued. "So we'll need to find Attena as soon as possible. Otherwise, we'll have to wait several days till it's safe to travel around the city again."

"So how do we find Attena?" asked Lara, who had begun helping Garbo clean off the table.

"I'll be right back," Hip said, heading for the apartment door. "I'll check for her work address at the library across the street. I'll be back in the blink of an eye."

Hip checked his watch, adjusted his glasses and grimaced. "But that still leaves us only a couple of hours before everything shuts down. Bianca, we may not be able to find Attena today – Zurbia is a big place."

"I'm sure we'll find her," Bianca said confidently.

Hip returned almost as quickly as promised. "Your mother is listed as the president of a business, Wisdom Inc. It's in downtown Zurbia. But we have to leave now to get there in time."

As Hip shoved Bianca and the others out the door, Garbo called out to them, "Come back, it's too late, you'll never make it."

CHAPTER 35

Going Up

"**D**o you think your mom's right about not having enough time to get there?" Jewel asked Hip as they ran down the apartment stairs.

"Could be," said Hip. "But we won't take the cycles. We'll take a taxi instead."

"A taxi?" Bianca asked. She glanced at Lara, to see if she knew what one was. Lara shrugged her shoulders.

"It's is a private car you hire to take you someplace," explained Hip.

"Sounds boring. I'd rather take your motorcycle," said Laser.

"Believe me, Laser, we'll be safer in a taxi," said Hip. He led them outside, waved his hands in the air and shouted taxi several times. A yellow car quickly pulled up in front of them.

Hip opened the two side doors. "Just hop in," he told his friends.

"You know we've never been in a car before," said Jewel, peering into the car and sniffing, as if she could smell danger.

"It's safe. You just sit inside and relax. The cabbie will do the rest," Hip assured them.

"Hey, Mack. What's going on?" asked the cabbie, turning to inspect his passengers.

A shiver went up Bianca's spine. For just a moment, his thick neck and curly red hair reminded Bianca of Mr. Backus.

"What's with these kids? They been locked up in a closet all their lives?" the cabbie snorted.

"They're just new to Zurbia. That's all," Hip replied.

"Well kick them in the butt. I can't wait all day. Vandals will be hitting the streets soon," the cabbie grumbled impatiently.

"OK, let's get in," suggested Lara and the others slid in after her.

"Just like I thought, it's like riding in a can," said Bianca to no one in particular. She rolled down her window and stuck her head out.

"Hey, kid. Get your fat head back inside or you'll get it knocked off by the next passing car," the cabbie yelled at her.

Bianca quickly withdrew her head and glared at the back of his thick bristly neck. He was the one with a fat head, not her, she mused.

It took more than an hour of driving past massive gray concrete buildings, with their endless rows of square windows. People walked quickly with their heads bent slightly as if staring at their feet and their eyes hidden beneath the brim of their hats. Men wore dark-blue suits, women dressed in gray ones.

The taxi dropped them in front of the Wisdom Inc. building. Several times higher than Tiara's palace, it towered above them. Twin ten-foot-high steel doors barred their entry. Off to the side sat a guard in a glass booth.

"I'd like to go in alone and visit Mom," Bianca told her friends.

"I see a coffee shop on the corner. We can wait there for you," said Hip. Its bright-red sign read, "Cafe Mars".

Bianca watched her friends walk down the street, and then turned to the guard who had stepped out of his booth. He wore a stern expression and a somber gray uniform. His cap rested just above two bushy black eyebrows. A small scab stuck out from the tip of his nose. How would Attena look? Had the acid rain affected her? she wondered.

"I'm here to visit my mother, Attena, President of Wisdom Inc.," she said boldly.

The guard looked Bianca over carefully. "What's your name?"

"Bianca," she said. After a moment, she said louder and more firmly, "Princess Bianca," hoping that her title might help her get inside.

"A princess, huh?" The guard raised his eyebrows. He

scanned a sheet of paper that he had pulled out of his pocket. "Well, I don't see any Princess Bianca on this list of people to be admitted," he said briskly.

A wave of anger washed over her. She glared at the guard: "I don't care about that stupid list. My mother works here and I'm going to see her."

"Big temper for a little girl. Well, I don't think you're a Vandal, so you can go inside. Attena is on the top floor, but you'll need this to see her." The guard handed her a crystal disk about the size of her fist.

"What is it?" Bianca asked.

"It's your key," he said.

She turned it over in her hands wondering how it worked, when the large doors swung open with barely a sound. Bianca looked up at the guard to ask about the key, but he was already back in his glass booth. She decided to get in quickly before the doors closed again.

Once inside, she found herself standing alone in a brightly lit lobby, barren of furniture. Its polished stainless-steel walls resembled a large tin box.

Across from the entrance were four doors without knobs. A red light blinked above one of them. Next to it was a small rectangular slot about the thickness of her disk.

Bianca's heart beat with anticipation as she walked up to the door and knocked on it. Nothing happened. She studied the slot and looked at her disk. Hesitantly, she slid the disk into the hole. It went in half way and the door slid open.

Bianca withdrew the disk and walked in. Another guard sat on a stool inside a very small room without windows.

"Going up?" he asked without smiling. His pale skin clung to his cheek bones like a wet sheet of paper.

Bianca was confused by his question. "I'm here to see Attena," she said peering back into the lobby, wondering if she should leave the tiny room. Just then the door slammed shut and the lobby was gone. She was trapped in the small space with the guard. It was far scarier than the forest.

The room shuddered for a moment, then the door slid open. She found herself looking into a different room. She timidly stepped out and a sharp clap sounded behind her. She spun around to face a solid wall of mirrors.

So many mirrors, it's like being in a ballet class, Bianca thought. Awkwardly she tried to balance herself on the tips of her toes. While tottering back and forth, she examined the skirt and blouse that Garbo had loaned her. I hope Mom likes them, she thought, she knows how much I dislike dressing up.

She studied the room in its reflection. It was very large and almost empty. A row of black leather chairs lined the brilliant white walls on either side of her like ebony keys on a piano.

Across the room from her were two huge purple doors. She turned to face them. Again there were no handles or knobs, but there was a slot.

This is all very odd, Bianca thought. Everything is so lifeless. Where are the people?

She walked up to the purple doors. Her fingers ran across their surface. They were as smooth as glass and as cold as ice. A chill went through her. Could this be the right place for Mom?

She clutched the crystal disk in her hand and felt butterflies in her stomach. Taking a deep breath, she slid the disk into the slot.

CHAPTER 36

Attena

The doors swished opened to Attena's office. Bianca withdrew the crystal disk and walked onto a smooth white marble floor. The walls were lined with rows of thick books.

At the far end of the room, against a wall of glass that looked out over Zurbia, was a black lacquer desk. Attena half sat on it with one foot touching the ground. She was reading a book and didn't notice Bianca's entrance.

The doors silently closed behind Bianca as she stood frozen, watching her mother. Everyone had said that Attena had died. And now, as if in a dream, her mother was before her.

Two separate feelings rushed through Bianca. She wanted to run laughing and crying into her mother's arms. But a quite different, stronger feeling stoked her anger.

Although her mother was as beautiful as she remembered, the Attena before her was cold, proper and distant. She still wore Tiara's royal purple head band, but the rest of her clothes were unlike any seen in Tiara. She wore a gray suit, tapered to just above her knees, with high-healed black shoes.

Those are not sensible shoes, thought Bianca. And that outfit! She looks like all the other dull people outside. What's happened? And she's ignoring me!

Bianca seethed, feeling small and insignificant, standing in the large, clean room. I've gone all this distance, I've nearly drowned, I've been chased by Vandals and she's just standing there! Reading a book!

Why didn't she come home? Tears streamed down Bianca's cheeks. She's become just like everything else here, uncaring. She doesn't care what's happened to me, or Dad or our home! Exploding, Bianca hurled the disk to the marble floor. With a loud, sharp crack, it shattered into a hundred tiny crystals.

As if a spell had been broken, Attena looked up with a start. The book slid from her hands to the floor. Bianca saw her mother's eyes turn glossy.

"Oh God," Attena said softly and approached her daughter.

For a moment Bianca stood frozen and then she raced across the room into her mother's arms. "You've been gone so long," she cried, digging her fingers into her mother's sides.

Still there was the anger. "Why didn't you come back?" Bianca shouted. But she didn't lessen her grip on Attena. No nightmare would sweep her mother away this time.

Attena whispered sweetly, "You're the most precious thing in the world to me. I can't believe you're here. I'd given up. I lost any feelings of happiness."

Her words washed away Bianca's anger. She felt her mother sobbing as they embraced for a long time.

Finally, Attena took Bianca by the shoulders and held her at arm's length. "Let me look at you," she said with a smile Bianca had only seen in her dreams for the past year. "You're so pretty."

Bianca blushed. "Mom, stop it. You're embarrassing me."

"But there's no one here but us." Attena laughed, then retrieved a small white handkerchief from her sleeve and gently dried Bianca's tears.

"I can't believe you're alive," Attena said, both laughing and crying.

"What do you mean?" Bianca asked. "We were told that you were dead!"

Attena looked shocked. "What?"

"We received a note from the king of Zurbia. It said that you had died trying to cross the Tygans."

Attena's face went pale. "You mean you never received my messages?"

"No," Bianca said slowly, remembering what Mr. Backus had said at the Last Inn. "I think your messengers must have been killed by the Vandals."

"So none of them made it to Tiara?" Attena asked.

"No. Dad was about to leave for Zurbia to find you when we received the note," Bianca said. "Now that I think of it, I never saw the messenger. I don't know who did. Maybe he was a Vandal working with Neechie."

"Neechie was working with the Vandals?" Attena asked incredulously.

"I think Bug used to be a Vandal or at least he hung out with them at the Last Inn. I heard some Vandals talking there. They said they passed on some information to Neechie that would make them all rich," explained Bianca.

"Do you know what they told him?" her mother asked.

"No, but I think they got the information from your messengers."

"They must have read my first note telling of the new mountain pass," said Attena, half to herself.

"What new pass?" Bianca asked.

"On the way to Zurbia, I studied the Tygans, trying to determine a better way to cross them. It took me almost two months but I finally came across a new pass," Attena replied.

"Is it big enough to build a road through?"

"Yes. It's much wider and much lower than the current one. But it's farther south, so it makes the journey longer."

"That's it!" Bianca exclaimed. "The Wizard wants to build a road through the pass you discovered so he can cut down the Tygan forest and sell the trees to Zurbia."

"He told you that?" Attena asked curiously.

"No, Dad and Zen did. They both told me that Neechie wanted to build a road over the Tygans but they said it would be impossible."

"Who's Zen?" asked Attena.

"He's Neechie's brother. He's a hermit that lives on this side of the Tygans," explained Bianca.

Attena sat back on her desk. She tapped her chin with a finger and looked at Bianca. "Neechie must have made up the message saying I had died. Then he sent another phony one to the

King of Zurbia saying that you and Rip had perished the same way."

"So you thought we were dead, too! But why didn't you return to Tiara?" asked Bianca, drawing nearer to Attena.

"I was so depressed, I couldn't bear the thought of living in Tiara without the two of you. I knew I should have returned to help your grandfather rule but being here does strange things to you. I felt myself being sucked into my work. Over time, my feelings went sort of dead. Memories of Tiara became fainter and returning there just kept being put off."

Attena let her fingers comb through Bianca's auburn hair as she observed, "I see Rip has been making sure you brush your hair." Then she looked puzzled and asked, "Where is Rip? Is he in the waiting room?"

"No...he's still in Tiara."

"What!" Attena exclaimed.

"Dad had just been crowned the new king when he got sick."

"Sick?" Attena said apprehensively.

"Actually Neechie slipped him a sleeping potion. Now Dad can't be wakened. And then Grandfather died that same night," Bianca explained.

Attena heaved a sorrowful sigh and was silent for a time. "I never thought of your grandfather ever dying." She wiped a tear from her eye. "I just expected him to go on forever, leading our little and peaceful kingdom. Obviously, I wasn't being realistic. And now he's dead and poor Rip is a prisoner of sleep."

"Neechie is ruling Tiara as my guardian and he's closed the palace off from everyone," said Bianca. "Just before Dad fell asleep he said I should come here. He must have read Neechie's mind with the Ruby Ring and found out you were alive."

Bianca squeezed Attena's arm and said, proudly "You'll get everything back to normal."

Overwhelmed by Bianca's tale, Attena said faintly, "Oh... I think I can."

CHAPTER 37

The Chamber

Attena took a deep breath and shook her head. "I feel like my whole life has just been given back to me. We must return to Tiara and find an antidote for Rip."

"Zen told me that a whiff from the Mir flowers would wake Dad, but he also said acid rain killed all of them," Bianca told her.

"I vaguely remember reading about the Mir plant, but I don't think we call it by that name," her mother said. "I'm sure we can find it somewhere," she added hopefully.

"So can we leave right away?" asked Bianca.

"Of course. I just have to meet with the Chamber."

"What's that?" Bianca asked impatiently.

"They're a group of citizens who are trying to change Zurbia," said Attena.

"Is it like a Town Council? Dad was going to call one and Neechie became really angry."

"These people would like to become a Town Council and be able to make rules," Attena explained. "In fact, it was at their suggestion that the King invited me to Zurbia. And although he needs their support, I've come to believe that he feels threatened by them and would like to see their efforts destroyed."

"Can he do that?" Bianca asked.

"Not directly. Even though many important people are members of the Chamber, they still often meet in secrecy. Vandals have broken up our public meetings. I suspect the King sends them to disrupt us. Tonight we have a secret meeting. I'll tell them I'm returning to Tiara."

Attena swung one leg over the other. Nervously she tapped her fingers on her knee.

"Bianca, there's so much to tell you... and, I still don't know how you got here. You obviously didn't come by yourself. Who did you come with?"

"I came with Lara. Then Laser and Jewel joined us," Bianca answered.

"Oh." Attena continued to tap her knee. "But who were the adults?"

"Mr. Popolo started out with us, but he had an accident and had to stay behind."

"And so, who were the other adults?"

"There weren't any." In some ways this was the best part of the story for Bianca. She liked seeing an adult's look of disbelief (like Zen and Hip, and now her mother's) upon discovering she and her friends had crossed the Tygan Mountains without any grownups.

Attena stopped tapping her knee. "Amazing!"

Bianca had been examining her mother's face for signs of pollution poisoning. "People told me that there's supposed to be lead and other poisons in the air," she said coyly.

"There are. You won't find any canaries in Zurbia," said Attena. "And yet my walls are lined with books listing all the ways to correct these problems."

She pointed out her office window. "Look at that building." Bianca strained her neck but couldn't see the top of it.

"That building is the largest in Zurbia. It's filled with lawyers. The King has hired thousands of them to make laws. And thousands more are hired by others to find ways around the laws."

"That seems like a waste of time," Bianca said as she gazed at all the thick, black books. She couldn't imagine reading all of them or wanting to. They looked so boring.

Turning back to her mother, she asked, "If there are so many laws, why are there so many Vandals?"

Attena sighed. "It doesn't make sense does it? Perhaps it's because the people who make the laws don't follow them. For instance, the King of Zurbia cares more about playing video games all day, or riding around in his limousine than caring for his people."

Bianca thought of the word Zen used. "He sounds as 'self-indulgent' as the Vandals."

"Yes, I guess so." Attena looked at Bianca curiously, surprised by her daughter's thoughtful observation.

"You have to be careful all the time. I don't know whether Zurbia is being harmed more by pollution or Vandals. Have they bothered you at all?" Attena asked.

"Yes, well, actually they were bothering Hip, not us. Oh ...," Bianca brought a hand up to her mouth. "I just remembered Hip and the rest are down at a coffee shop, waiting for us."

"Cafe Mars on the corner?" Attena asked, anxiously.

"Yes."

"That's a hangout for Vandals!" Attena jumped off her desk, grabbed Bianca's hand, practically dragging her through the purple doors and across to the wall of mirrors. She pushed a button and the wall opened up to reveal the tiny room again.

"What is this place?" Bianca asked, as they stepped into the windowless room.

Attena chuckled, "It's an elevator. Tiara doesn't have any because no building is over three stories tall."

The doors opened onto the lobby. "Later, we'll talk about elevators and other Zurbian wonders," Attena promised as they dashed out of the building toward Cafe Mars.

CHAPTER 38

Cafe Mars

Bianca and Attena found Cafe Mars empty but for Bianca's friends. A few feet from the entrance, Laser was playing a video game. The others were sitting at the back of a long room filled with a dozen small tables.

"Attena, we thought you were dead!" shouted Laser.

"I'm very much alive," Attena said and threw her arm around him.

Jewel rushed over and hugged Attena. "You've got to get back to Tiara. The Wizard's taken over. He won't let Mom and Dad leave the palace," she blurted out.

"The Wizard's days are numbered," Attena assured them.

Lara came over next to embrace Attena. "Without your help, Bianca wouldn't have made it," Attena said. "I owe a lot to you."

Lara shrugged. "That's what friends are for."

Attena then looked at Hip, standing beside Lara, and asked, "And who is your friend?"

Before Lara could say anything, Hip reached out and shook Attena's hand vigorously. "I'm their tour guide," he said, grinning, and then offered her a chair at their table. Laser, however, stayed behind at the video game.

After they sat down, Attena cautioned them, "We shouldn't stay here too long. Almost no one comes here but Vandals."

"I was wondering if this place served bad food," said Lara, looking around the empty cafe.

"But they do have a video game, and I'm going to beat Laser before we leave," said Jewel, leaving the table to join him.

Before she reached her brother, three unshaven thugs about Hip's age strolled into the cafe. They wore soiled white T-shirts and tight black jeans. Laser continued exploding alien space ships, oblivious to them.

"Hey, kid. Beat it. This is our video game," the ugliest one said, tapping him on the shoulder. Laser turned around. Three scab-covered faces glared down at him.

"I was here first," Laser weakly protested.

The Vandals looked at each other and laughed. "Should we stand in line?" said the ugliest Vandal, a menacing grin on his face. He grabbed Laser's hair and lifted him off the ground. "You're going to the back of line, buster." Laser yelled and tried to hit the Vandal.

"Put my brother down!" Jewel yelled and ran toward them. She scooped up a cup from a table and pitched it at the Vandal's head. It bounced off but drew blood. The Vandal dropped Laser and felt his wound.

Bianca and the others charged to the front of the room. Jewel stood motionless, apparently stunned by her feat. Attena grabbed her arm and raced for the door.

Bianca rushed to Laser. He was dazed but still on his feet. They quickly side-stepped the nearest Vandal and flew past the others and out of the cafe.

Hip and Lara blocked the door from the pursuing Vandals. The ugliest one, blood trickling down the side of his head, lunged at them.

Hip defiantly stretched out his open hands, as if trying to halt traffic. His voice was loud but its trembling betrayed him. "Back off, mister. We're on our way out."

The Vandal scornfully brushed Hip's arms aside and socked him.

A second later, Lara smacked the Vandal's head with a sweeping leg kick. The Vandal stumbled backward into the cafe's window and screamed as he smashed through it. Lara whirled around and pushed the stunned Hip toward the door. He stumbled out, holding his jaw in pain.

Another Vandal took a swing at Lara. She ducked his blow and caught his arm. With a quick jerk she sent him sailing through the air. With a loud thud, he landed on a thick wooden table and lifelessly slid to the floor.

The third Vandal slowly backed away and held up his hands, as if surrendering. Lara eyed him closely. Then she glanced at the other Vandal on the floor. Both wore a single silver star earring. Lara glared at the third Vandal. "Where did you get that earring?" she demanded.

The Vandal, caught off guard, was tongue-tied. Lara clenched her fists and stepped toward him. He backed further away. "Our boss hands them out," he replied.

"Who is he?" she pressed.

"His name is Rand, and when he finds out about this rumble, you're dead meat!" he spat out.

"What does he look like?" Lara pressed.

"Stick around and find out for yourself." Feeling more confident, the Vandal laughed. He then grabbed a mug from the counter and threw it at Lara's head. She caught it on the fly, wound up and let it rip. It caught him between the eyes. He went down like a felled tree.

Bianca called from the doorway, "Lara let's go. The rest are safely in Attena's office building."

Lara surveyed the blood-splattered cafe. "I wonder what they do for fun around here?" she joked.

CHAPTER 39

Staying Behind

Bianca and Lara found Laser in the lobby gently rubbing the top of his head. Hip stood nearby holding a swollen jaw. Attena had felt his jaw and decided it wasn't broken. She suggested he take a taxi home and left to ask the guard to hail one.

As she walked away, Lara spoke to Bianca, "Now that you've found Attena, I'm sure you'll make it back to Tiara safely," matter-of-factly.

"Lara," Bianca's voice quavered. "What do you mean? Aren't you coming with us?

"No, I'm staying here," Lara said, looking determined.

"Why? It's dangerous. You'll be killed." Her own words reminded her of Jewel's similar warning about traveling to Zurbia.

"Bianca," Lara hugged her friend tightly. She spoke softly, "I just want what you have: a family." Lara bit her lip and hesitated. "I've always had this lingering feeling that maybe Dad hadn't been killed by the Vandals. You know how some said he joined them. It was something I never wanted to think about. But now ... I know he's here, in Zurbia."

Bianca's eyes opened wide. "How do you know?"

"Dad used to make silver star earrings for Mom. I still have a pair. The Vandals at the coffee shop had earrings just like them."

A lump grew in Bianca's throat. "What does that mean? Anyone could make that kind of earring."

"Perhaps. But Mom's nickname for Dad was Rand," Lara said.

Bianca had heard the Vandal say their boss' name was Rand. She knew Lara would not return until she tracked down this person Rand.

Lara swung her arm around Bianca's shoulders and gave her another hug. "We'll see each other again. I have to do this. Please understand."

Bianca couldn't speak. As hard as she tried, she couldn't swallow that lump in her throat. Her eyes went watery. Lara had been loyal and now Bianca felt like she was abandoning her. "We should stay and help you find him," she said.

"You can't. You must go home and finish what you set off to do. But my own mission is just beginning," said Lara.

Bianca knew she was right, but still, there was something unfair about losing a close friend just when she had found her mom.

Attena returned and told Hip a taxi had arrived. "I've paid him to take you directly home. You should leave now before there are more partying Vandals on the streets."

Hip shook Attena's hand and turned to Bianca. He reached into his pocket and took out a small piece of paper. Though it was obviously painful to talk, he mumbled, "This is my address. Should you ever come back, please stay with me and my family."

He then gave each of them a hug. When he came to Lara, she stopped him. "You don't have to hug me good-bye."

Hip looked puzzled.

"I'm staying in Zurbia for awhile. Could you put me up for a short time?"

Hip tried to smile, but it was too painful. Instead, he nodded.

"Lara, what are you saying?" Attena asked.

"I have to stay here."

"She has to find her dad and she thinks he's living in Zurbia," Bianca explained.

"I understand, but we can't stay with you. We must get back to Tiara," Attena said.

"Yes, I know," Lara said with a smile.

"If you need help, contact the Chamber. Tell them that I sent you. I'm sure Hip knows about them."

Lara thanked Attena and gave each of her fellow travelers a hug. She kissed Bianca on the cheek. "I'll always think of you as my sister."

With an aching heart, Bianca watched Lara and Hip walk into the waiting taxi. Attena squeezed her hand and whispered, "We'll see Lara again."

Attena then announced that she had to go upstairs to notify the Chamber she was leaving. "They won't be happy," she added, frowning.

When the elevator reached Attena's floor, Jewel and Laser stayed behind in the waiting room. Bianca followed her mother into the meeting room.

CHAPTER 40

So Long Zurbia

Adozen stern adults sat around a large oval table. Dressed in suits of varying shades of gray, they looked far too serious for Bianca. They probably hadn't had any fun for a long time.

There was an empty chair saved for Attena. A woman sitting nearest Attena's spot asked Bianca, "May I get you a chair?"

"No thank you. We won't be staying long," Bianca replied and crossed her fingers.

The Chamber members began murmuring among themselves. Bianca heard one or two ask, "Who is she?"

The talking stopped when Attena rapped the table with her knuckles. She stood by her seat, and in a clear, strong voice, announced, "This is my daughter, Bianca. She crossed over the Tygan Mountains to bring me home." Attena placed her arm around Bianca and continued, "I'll be leaving this evening."

Bianca heard someone whisper to another, "She can't leave, there's work to do."

"I set out to help the people of Zurbia. I think I have, in some small way," Attena said.

Before she could go on, a young man interrupted her. "Attena, we've just begun making changes. Your work is here. Have your daughter stay with you. There are a thousand more things to do in Zurbia than Tiara."

Attena raised her hand for silence. "My kingdom is in danger, I must return to Tiara."

An old stoop-shouldered man interrupted: "Tiara is of the past. Zurbia is the future. It may seem to be an ugly, scary future, but unless we reshape it, it will spread like cancer across the mountains into your cherished little kingdom. From what you've told us, each year more and more Vandals raid your valley. How long will it be before they breach your wall or decide to stay all year long in your valley?"

The image of Vandals roaming Tiara year round, not just in the summer, stunned Bianca. Could that really happen? All the more reason to get Attena back to topple the Wizard and to defend Tiara. Bianca gently poked her elbow into Attena's side. Attena whispered back, "Don't worry. I won't stay."

"We should leave now," Bianca said impatiently.

More Chamber members argued strongly for Attena to stay. But a few others understood her need to return. Bianca continued to prod Attena, as the words continued, piling up like the papers on Rip's desk. Adults took so long to make up their minds.

But one by one, each person eventually gave in to Attena's arguments. Just like home, thought Bianca – Mom always won her arguments against Dad.

Afterwards, Attena and Bianca joined their friends in the waiting room. "We have to move quickly," said Attena. "Soon Vandals will be forcing everyone off the streets. We'll take a taxi to the outskirts of town. There is a stable there with riding horses."

"I can't ride a horse dressed in this," said Jewel, referring to her pleated skirt.

"Don't worry," said Attena, as she led them down to catch a taxi. "There are riding clothes available at the stable for Bianca and you."

Jewel nervously looked up and down the street.

"Is something wrong?" Attena asked her.

"Shouldn't we travel with others for protection?"

"Perhaps, but there isn't time to round up others and all of my original guards are gone. They either died in the forest fighting Vandals or returned to Tiara as messengers. But we can make it. Our horses are fast and more agile than motorcycles for crossing the mountains."

"What about supplies?" asked Laser.

"There's a cabin in the foothills where we can spend the first night. It's always stocked with supplies and we can take some for our journey," Attena replied.

It was early evening now. With each passing minute, more cycles roared onto the streets.

Bianca pressed her face against the taxi window. At some street corners, huge bonfires spewed out thick black columns of smoke. People danced wildly around them, drinking from bottles and shouting at their passing taxi.

"What are they burning?" Bianca asked, as she watched the gray sky turn black.

"They're burning old tires to celebrate the beginning of the holiday," said Attena.

"Boy, they're really stinking this place up," said Jewel, wrinkling her nose at the awful stench.

"We're leaving this all behind us. Soon we'll be riding across the plain," said Attena, taking in her last view of Zurbia's mad dance of "freedom".

At the stable, they mounted four well-groomed horses. Attena led the way across the desolate landscape.

Bianca rode next to Attena. "I've been meaning to tell you something, Mom," she began hesitantly. "When Dad told me to come here, I didn't think I could do it at first." Bianca paused. "I knew I'd need some special help in getting here."

"You chose your traveling companions well," Attena replied.

"I was talking about something else," Bianca said sheepishly.

"What?" Attena looked puzzled.

Bianca gulped. "I took the Ruby Ring with me."

"You did?" Attena arched her eyebrows in surprise.

Anxiety knotted Bianca's stomach. Would her mother forgive her? "And, I lost it," she said with unexpected firmness. "There I said it. I feel horrible, but I needed it to save Jewel from drowning. And then I dropped the Ruby Ring in the river. Now it's lost forever."

Attena became silent. She stared into the distance, lost in thought and perhaps memories of the past. A tear ran down her cheek.

Bianca wondered if her mother was remembering how the Ruby Ring looked long ago on Grandfather. Those were happier days. Now the Ruby was gone and the King was dead. Would Tiara ever be the same?

Slowly, Attena smiled. "We all try to do our best. That's all anyone can ask; even when we fail or fall short. You did what was right. Tiara will have to survive through our human efforts, without the Ruby Ring, and without our kind, old King."

Bianca felt a sense of relief, things would work out. They were going home, that's what mattered most. She swung around on her saddle for one last look at Zurbia. Behind her great pillars of black smoke formed a dense cloud above the city, blocking out the sun and leaving only a single golden thread to outline its dark mass.

But then she saw something else: a bank of billowing dust moving toward them.

"What's that?" Bianca drew Attena's attention to it.

"I'd say it was a large number of motorcycles forming a straight line across the plain. Cars would keep to the road. It's strange though. Why would they be leaving the city at this time? They should be celebrating in the city," said Attena.

She studied the dust cloud for a moment and then added in a worried tone, "They could catch up with us before we reach the hills."

Attena called out to Jewel and Laser, who were riding ahead. "Looks like Vandals behind us."

Jewel and Laser turned in their saddles and took in the scene.

Attena spoke calmly. "We'll be OK if we make it to the foothills. Once there, we can lose them and get to the cabin." Without further discussion, they spurred the horses toward the foothills.

In their trail a hundred cycles stretched across the plain, the distant roar of their engines becoming ever louder.

CHAPTER 41

Surrounded

The road became windy and narrow as Bianca and the others galloped into the foothills. After a couple of miles they left it to ride cross-country through light underbrush and groves of scrawny pine trees.

"We should lose them now. Our horses are faster than their cycles in this terrain," Attena said and checked her watch. "We should reach the cabin within an hour or so."

Mom never wore a watch before, observed Bianca. She's picked up the Zurbian habit of always measuring time. It's almost as if there is less of it here than in Tiara, or that it's more valuable here, something that you wouldn't waste.

Before nightfall, they reached the cabin. They went without a fire so the Vandals wouldn't see their smoke.

As they settled in for the night, Bianca worried about crossing the Tygans. "Mom, getting back to Tiara is going to be difficult. There could be Vandals waiting for us on the other side."

"I'm sure we can get by them," Attena said. But her brave smile seemed forced.

Bianca tossed and turned during the night, thinking of the dangers ahead. Eros promised to fly them to Tiara if they returned to the Cave of Wishes. But she wasn't sure how to find it. And even if she did, she couldn't call Eros to meet them, since she had lost the Ruby Ring.

A draft of chilly morning air snuck under her covers, sending shivers up her spine. She rolled over on her side and saw Attena looking out the window. "Let's start a fire. I'm cold," said Bianca.

Attena turned away from the window and frowned.

"What's the matter?" Bianca asked.

"The Vandals have tracked us down," she replied. "I stayed

up most of the night to be on guard, but they must have come on foot because I never heard their cycles. When dawn came they were already camped outside."

Bianca gasped. Not even Lara could have helped them now. She threw off the covers and joined her mother at the window. Jewel and Laser were still asleep.

Outside, about a dozen scruffy Vandals were sitting around drinking beers.

"I wonder where the rest of them are?" said Bianca.

"It looks like they're waiting for the rest of their gang or their leader," Attena whispered back. "I think I recognize one of the Vandals from the coffee shop."

As Bianca examined the thugs, she noticed the sunlight reflecting off their star-shaped earrings. "Yes, I recognize one of them. They're also wearing the same earrings the Vandals wore at the coffee shop," she said.

Attena looked at her daughter. "That's very observant of you." She rested her chin in her hand, thinking. "They must have followed us out of the city to get revenge for Lara beating up their buddies."

"They probably didn't see her leave with Hip," Bianca added.

Suddenly an even larger group of Vandals, led by one on a big black cycle, roared into the Vandal encampment. The cabin shook and Laser stirred. "What was that?" he asked, yawning. He rubbed his eyes and stumbled over to the window.

"Oh no. More Vandals!" Laser moaned.

The lead motorcyclist dismounted while the other Vandals ran up and slapped him on the back.

He was taller than the rest and had a dark thick beard. His sleeveless black leather jacket revealed a large tattoo on his right arm but Bianca couldn't make out what it was.

"Mom, can you see his tattoo?"

"Yes, it says Rand," she replied.

Bianca's heart skipped a beat. It must be Lara's dad. She had to speak to him.

Jewel finally awoke and sat up in bed. "What's going on?" she asked.

No one replied.

"Why does everyone look so worried? Are there Vandals outside?" she asked anxiously.

"I think we'll need a kitchen full of coffee cups. How far can you throw?" Laser quipped.

Bianca left the window. "I'm going out to talk to him."

"What! You are doing no such thing!" said Attena.

"You don't understand. That's Lara's dad..." Bianca tried to explain but was cut off by Attena.

"He may have been at one time, but he's a Vandal now."

"Mother," Bianca said in a determined tone. "I got here safely. Didn't I?"

"Yes, of course, but now ..." Attena began.

"Look, they obviously can come in here whenever they want to. At least if I talk to him, maybe ..."

"Attena, let her go," Laser begged. "It's worth a try."

Before Attena could reply, Bianca opened the cabin door and was striding toward the leader of the Vandals.

CHAPTER 42

Redemption

R and's back was to Bianca. As she approached him, the Vandals facing her stopped their loud chatter, causing Rand to swing around.

His expression was that of a dead man's, without a touch of warmth or flicker of life. His dark eyes were like two deep, bottomless wells, as if his soul had been buried long ago from the living world.

Bianca felt as if she were walking into a morgue: a dead forest for a waiting room and a pack of ghouls as guests. The crisp morning air only served to etch their evil glares into her heart.

"We're here to finish a fight," Rand growled in a deep, low voice that seemed to echo from within him.

"It was your daughter who finished it," Bianca retorted. Surprisingly, she felt at ease.

He leaned back and studied Bianca. His black eyes bore into her like the Wizard's had.

"She died long ago," he snapped.

"She didn't die," Bianca said. Then she noticed his ruby earring. It reminded her of the rubies that the Wood Nymphs wore. That is, all except for Pyx.

Suddenly Bianca made the connection. The other Nymphs said Pyx had done something she shouldn't have. She must have given her ruby to the Vandal who had spared her life.

And now she stood before him. Was it possible that some kindness still flickered deep within the darkness of this stranger; this Vandal who once lived in Tiara and was the father of Lara. Or had Zurbia changed him forever?

"You know I'm telling the truth, don't you?" she challenged him, trying to stir old memories, trying to reach out to his past.

Rand drew back, his jaw dropped slightly. "Who are you?"

he demanded.

"She's my daughter," said Attena, stepping up behind Bianca.

Before Rand could say another word, Bianca asked, "You got your ruby earring from a Wood Nymph, didn't you?"

Some of the Vandals laughed. But Rand didn't. His rough hands trembled slightly as he scratched his beard.

"She said you were different from the rest," said Bianca, hoping it was still true.

The Vandals began murmuring among themselves. Bianca heard one say, "What's with this kid? Does she have something on Rand we don't know about?"

A quick glare from Rand silenced them. He turned his attention back to Bianca, and asked sharply, "If my daughter is alive, where is she?"

Eyeing the Vandals that surrounded them, Attena spoke up. "How can we trust you? If Bianca tells you where your daughter is, what's to stop your gang from killing us?"

A slight smile of respect crossed his face. "OK, I understand your concern." He turned and told the Vandal nearest him, "Take the gang back to Zurbia, I can handle this by myself."

The Vandal motioned to the others to mount their bikes. Soon the ground beneath Bianca's feet shook as the cycles roared off into the dying forest. She glanced back at the cabin. Laser and Jewel had their faces pressed against the window.

Within a few minutes the rest of Vandals had driven off.

"I'm not as bad as you think I am," Rand said slowly. "I've had anything I desired in Zurbia ... except the return of my family."

His dark, deep eyes flickered for the first time. Behind this death mask, a soul seemed to be stirring.

"Why did you leave Lara?" Bianca asked.

Rand was silent for a moment, as if mustering his courage. When he finally spoke, it was with great sadness. "I was drunk and carelessly started the fire that burned down my home. I was barely conscious when the Vandals found me lying outside. When I realized what I had done, I felt so ashamed of myself. I couldn't face the thought of others pointing at me and saying, 'That drunk killed his family.' So, I left with the Vandals. I didn't deserve a better life."

He stared down at his feet. "All these years I've been alone. Now you tell me that my daughter is alive. If that could only be true." It was a voiced tinged with hope, with lost feelings and new-found emotions.

"We need to get to the Cave of Wishes. If you help us get there, I'll tell you ... how to find your daughter," said Bianca, weighing her words. How did she feel about this stranger. Should she really trust him?

Rand looked up at them. "If this is a trick, none of you will leave this side of the mountains alive," he threatened. "You know I can read your thoughts."

"I know," Bianca said, sure and steady, not a heart beat missed.

"Bianca, we can't trust him. He's a Vandal," cautioned Attena. "And he's not going to change now."

"Why not? Anyone can change if they want to."

"Bianca, it's not like magic. People don't change by waving a wand over them."

"But it is magic! And it's not done with a wand. It comes from ... from within, from your heart."

Rand seemed to ignore their discussion as he scratched his beard. Finally he snorted, as if he could care less about their problems. "OK, I'll take you to this cave. I know how to get there but it's a long way off, on a rough, desolate part of the mountains. Even with horses it'll take us two days."

Attena sighed and looked at Bianca. "I hope you're right about him." Then she said in a commanding voice, "Let's get moving. We can make a quick breakfast and be out of here in an hour." On the way to the cabin, she asked Bianca, "Why in the world should we go to this cave?"

"I hope to contact a friend there," said Bianca, smiling.

"What kind of friend lives in a cave?"

"He doesn't actually live in the cave. I really don't know where he lives."

Attena only looked more perplexed.

"It's a long story, Mom, I'll explain later."

After they ate, Attena gave Rand one of the larger horses, and had Jewel and Laser double up.

All day and into the early evening they followed the river Styx upstream. Their horses carefully plodded up a steep rocky path that bordered the waterfall they had plunged down.

Late in the day they reached the marsh where the rowboat had been hidden. From there, they rode beside the stream that led to Zen's cabin, which they reached at dusk.

But they were greeted only with smoldering ruins. The roof was caved in and the side walls had been reduced to charred logs and smashed rocks. Zen's pipe lay on the ground outside, but there was no sign of him. They immediately searched the area for him.

Soon, from a nearby clump of bushes, Jewel yelled out, "Hurry! He's over here."

They all rushed to where the old man lay, near death. His eyes were swollen shut and his frail, bloodied hands weakly searched the ground around him.

Attena knelt and cradled his head in her lap. He spoke softly. "Vandals... They wanted valuables, but I had none... "

His chest heaved with each word spoken.

Tears flowed down Bianca's cheeks as she knelt beside him. "Why did they do this? Why?"

Zen reached out and touched her hand. "Greed... It blinds one's heart..."

He coughed slightly. "Take my ring..."

Bianca slid off a plain band made of cherry wood. Her tears fell onto his open palm.

"I know it's you, Bianca... Give this ring to my brother... He'll recognize it...Tell him that all life is precious... to love and protect it in memory of me..." Zen let out a gasp and was gone.

They were silent for a time, not knowing what to say. Then Rand returned to the ruined cabin and found a shovel lying on the ground. He dug a grave, and in silence buried the wise, old man.

It was a gloomy, starless night. The smoldering remains of Zen's cabin provided them with a campfire, but there wasn't much talk as they ate the rations Attena had brought.

A chill wind blew sparks from the fire high above their heads. Bianca watched the tiny, glowing points of light sail into the ocean of blackness. She thought about Zen and his kindness.

Across the campfire sat Rand. Bianca studied his face, framed against the night by a bright, yellowish glow from the fire. He never blinked, as if hypnotized by the flames. He seemed to be in another world as surely as poor Zen was.

Bianca searched Rand's face trying to understand him. Should she give this cold and distant man Lara's address? But then again, he was Lara's father and she wanted to find him. Could he change or would he always be a Vandal?

Rand suddenly looked up at Bianca and startled her. She realized that he had been reading her mind. "I hope there's love in your heart," she thought.

His eyes were as sad as any she'd ever seen. He got up abruptly and walked into the darkness.

The fire had turned to crackling embers. Jewel and Laser were fast asleep. Attena put her arm around Bianca and said, "It's time to sleep, we have a long journey ahead of us tomorrow."

Bianca nodded and huddled next to her. "I think Rand is trying to find his feelings," she said.

"I hope he does, because there are Vandals out there and we need his help," Attena replied.

Bianca peered into the night, wondering if Rand would still be with them in the morning.

CHAPTER 43

The Awakening

When Bianca awoke at dawn, she was relieved to see Rand packing their horses for the trip up the steep slope to the cave. It was a long, dry, silent journey, and by the time they reached the cave, the sun had set. Behind them, its last rays painted the horizon a bright crimson. A half-moon shone in the eastern sky.

"Let's rest in the cave," Attena suggested, dismounting. She drew Bianca aside and asked "When do we meet your friend?"

Bianca had to contact Eros somehow. She held her mother's hand and said, "Pretty soon, I hope."

Rand approached them. "I've kept my half of the bargain. Now keep your half." He didn't look nearly as tired as the rest of them.

"You kept your promise, but I have another favor to ask," said Bianca.

Rand looked suspiciously at Bianca. "I'm not in the habit of trusting anyone." He sighed and then quietly asked, "What is it?"

"I need to hold your ruby earring," she said.

"That's impossible! I never take it off. It protects me from treachery." He folded his arms across his chest defiantly.

"Without the ruby, we can't get back," Bianca said desperately.

"Look, mister," said Laser, "Lara stayed in Zurbia to find you because she thought you might be alive. But we don't want to stay here. We just want to go home with Attena. We won't steal your ruby. Bianca just wants to hold it. She can do things with it."

"What things?" Rand asked.

"I don't know. But she got us here and she can get us back," said Laser.

Rand studied Bianca as if he were trying to read her mind.

Then he slowly removed his earring. He lifted her hand and placed the ruby in her palm, gently closing her fingers around it.

She was going home – if the ruby worked. Her heart beat excitedly. Her "thank you" was but a dry whisper.

Clasping the ruby, Bianca shut her eyes and thought of Eros "Please come and get us. Take us back to Tiara."

Attena and the others were silent. An occasional dripping of water from inside the cave echoed against its rocky walls.

Bianca opened her eyes and searched the sky. The stars were now out and the moon was glowing. But there was no Eros.

Attena whispered to Jewel, "What is she looking for?"

"I think she's trying to call Eros. This is where he left us."

"Eros? Who's Eros?" Attena asked Jewel, in a hushed voice.

Before she could answer, Jewel jumped up and yelled, "There he is!"

The moon's rays shimmered on the huge wings of Eros as he soared across the sky. Attena stood, her mouth agape. Bianca heard her mother whisper. "I can't believe this."

Eros's hoofs barely touched the ground as he drifted into the mouth of the cave. "I'm at your service," the stallion said.

"Thank you for coming. We need your help. Can you take us back to Tiara?" Bianca urgently directed her thoughts to Eros

"Of course. You'll find yourself home when the sun rises."

Bianca turned to the others and cried out, "We can leave now! We'll be in Tiara by morning."

Attena helped Laser and Jewel mount Eros.

Bianca reached into her pocket and took out a piece of paper with Hip's address on it. She would have shuddered at the thought of giving it to a Vandal, but she felt that Rand was different now. He cared for someone else besides himself. She handed it to him. * "Lara is staying with a family. The young man is named Hip. He's a librarian. Lara saved him from a group of Vandals who were going to beat him up."

She searched Rand's eyes and added, "Perhaps they would have killed him, like Zen."

Rand sighed and then frowned. Bianca wasn't sure if he was angry or thankful. He reached out and took the paper. As he looked down at the address, he shook his head slowly.

"I feel like I'm going home too," he said. A weak smile crossed his face.

"Here's your earring back. Thank you." Bianca held the ruby in her outstretched palm.

Rand closed her hand around it for the second time. "It's yours. I won't be needing it. I no longer need to control a gang of Vandals. I just need to get my own life under control."

He walked back to the horses and mounted his. He grabbed the reins of the others and said, "I'll see that they're well cared for."

Bianca waved good-bye as he rode away. She cried out, "Tell Lara I love her and to come back to Tiara."

"I promise you'll see her again," Rand shouted back.

Attena put her arm around Bianca. "It's time to go home and wake up your dad."

"Do you think we can?"

"I'm sure we can," Attena said.

They then climbed onto Eros, who gracefully slipped into the sky. Within a few minutes they were soaring across the Tygans.

Bianca held the ruby in her hand. Although she loved its warmth, she wouldn't be keeping it.

"Mom, I'm giving this ruby back to Pyx."

"Who's Pyx?" Attena asked.

"She's a Wood Nymph. She gave her ruby to Rand because he spared her life."

"A Wood Nymph? I never would have thought I'd be meeting a Wood Nymph or a flying horse," Attena laughed.

"It's true," Bianca said. "There is magic in the world." And, she thought, I found it.

But in the morning, Bianca would still have to face the Wizard's magic.

CHAPTER 44

Black Magic is No Magic

The first thing Bianca noticed was the crisp air, tingling her cheeks. She opened her eyes to the bluest morning sky she had ever seen.

Eros silently swooped into an empty, quiet plaza; the people of Tiara had yet to rise.

"I will be off now," said Eros, as his passengers slid off his back. "City life, no matter how small the city, makes me nervous. I prefer the forest and mountains."

"Will I see you again?" Bianca asked, patting his head one last time.

"In time we will all meet again. Your life has just begun." The great stallion's powerful wings gently lifted him into the sky.

She had been a reluctant adventurer, but now that her quest had come to an end, there was a slight feeling of emptiness. As she watched Eros soar over Tiara's wall, her thoughts were interrupted by Laser.

"I'm going to see Dad, catch you later, Bianca," he said and ran off toward the palace.

"Wait for me," cried Jewel, running after him.

As Laser and Jewel swung open the palace doors, Bianca heard two guards groaning, caught sleeping on their watch. Laser and Jewel ran past them before they could get to their feet.

"Bianca, those are beautiful flowers blooming in your window box. What do you call them?" Attena asked, pointing to Bianca's spire.

"You know. Those are Pax flowers."

"Yes, but on the other side of the Tygans they were called Mir flowers," her mother said.

Bianca's mouth opened wide and then she broke into a huge grin. "Those flowers can wake up Dad!"

"Yes. I recalled seeing them somewhere. But I couldn't remember where until we flew into the plaza."

Excited, Bianca dashed toward the palace, without saying another word.

The guards had finally risen. One grabbed Bianca's sleeve as she tried to step past him. "Just a minute. We have instructions to hold on to you."

"Who said?" Bianca protested, struggling to pull her arm away.

"The Wizard," said the other.

Just then, the Wizard came running down the hallway toward her. "Don't let her go," he cried.

A moment later he stood next to her, slightly wheezing but looking smug. "So I see you wisely gave up your adventure and returned. Now hand over the Ruby Ring."

Attena walked up behind Bianca. The guards immediately stepped back. The Wizard looked up from Bianca and, seeing Attena, his arrogance melted in her glare.

"We all thought you were dead," he stammered.

"That's what you would have everyone believe. Your lies have been uncovered. Guards, arrest him," ordered Attena.

The guards hesitated. The Wizard took advantage of their indecision. He quickly drew his arms around himself and stepped back, his eyes darted from side to side.

"Don't anyone step near me – or you'll pay dearly." His voice was strong but desperate.

"Your threats are meaningless," Attena said.

Bianca wondered if Neechie's threat was real.

"Judge for yourself," he said and flung his arms wide again. A cloud of smoke suddenly engulfed him and the entire hallway.

The guards yelled in surprise but Attena spoke calmly. "Smoke can't hide your crimes."

The smoke soon disappeared into the air and apparently so had the Wizard.

"It's his magic," cried one of the guards.

Bianca would not be tricked again. He must be hiding somewhere, she thought. But he couldn't have gone very far. Her eyes scanned the hallway for clues and settled upon the broom closet a few feet away.

She walked over to it, placed her hand on the doorknob, and flung the door open.

Sandwiched inside was the Wizard, his robes drawn tightly around himself. Framed between two mop heads, he grinned sheepishly. The gig was up.

The Wizard coolly stepped out of the closet, brushed himself off as if nothing had happened. He cleared his voice. "Attena, please believe me when I tell you that I didn't mean to do any harm. I could've changed Tiara for the better. We could've become a modern city. And we could've all become rich!"

"How? Being like Zurbia? They've got Vandals everywhere. They've ruined their forest and they kill for greed," said Bianca.

"Oh Bianca, child. You exaggerate." The Wizard tried sounding fatherly.

"Your brother didn't think so. He wanted you to have this." Bianca handed Zen's wooden ring to the Wizard.

For the first time in Bianca's memory, Neechie actually looked sad. His lips trembled as he fingered the ring in his palm.

"He's dead, isn't he?"

"The Vandals killed him. He told us that all life was precious. And he asked that you protect it."

The Wizard hung his head. "He could have become rich and powerful, but he sought only harmony with nature. It's something that I've never valued." He looked up at them. "I thought everyone would be happier, if they listened to me. I have seen the future. And it will come crashing down on this Kingdom like an avalanche."

Attena shook her head. "You've only seen one future, one that worships power, the power to always obtain more, to always feed one's desires. Your modern Tiara would be built on conquering nature.

"We follow another path. One that respects nature and our fellow citizens. We control our desires so that they do not control us," she said.

The Wizard nodded slowly. He would not argue. But had he repented?

"From this day forward you are banished from our town," she declared.

The Wizard swallowed hard. "What shall I do? I can't go back to Zurbia. The Vandals will kill me. I've promised them a fortune. When they find out I have nothing to give them..." His trembling hands pressed together begging for mercy.

Attena smiled. "However, I'll let you stay in our valley, shoveling cow manure and husking corn. You can learn how to create wealth from nature rather than destroying it to seek wealth."

Bianca was still upset. "How do you expect to wake my dad. I know you gave him the sleeping potion."

The Wizard shook his head. "I can't wake him. I'm sorry. I don't know of any antidote."

"You're not such a Wizard after all," Bianca said with a great amount of satisfaction. She ran past him, down the hallway, and up to her room. There, she plucked out a Pax flower from her window box and raced to Rip's room.

Bianca knelt down by her father's side, holding the blossom.

As Rip inhaled the strong aroma of the Pax flower, his eyes opened slowly. Groggily he whispered, "Bianca."

She wrapped her arms around him and cried, "Dad, I missed you."

Rip looked confused. He rubbed his eyes and spoke slowly, "The last thing I remember is being crowned king. But I feel like I've been asleep for 20 years."

"No, just over a week," said Bianca wiping the tears from her eyes and laughing joyfully.

Rip stretched out his arms and yawned. "What happened? Who took care of you?"

"Well, I've had an adventure."

"An adventure?" Rip looked doubtfully at Bianca. "Real or imaginary?"

"A real one! A very real one," Bianca insisted.

"But there was a little magic in it, too," said Attena as she walked into the bedroom and hugged an astonished Rip.

T H E   E N D

ABOUT THE AUTHOR

Nick Licata started telling tales in grade school to his schoolmates on campouts. Later, as a father he spun tales for his daughter at bed time. As he grew bolder he told them in public and soon thereafter was elected to public office, where he continues to spin tales.

As a writer his first pieces were published as political columns in his college newspaper at Bowling Green State University. After moving to Seattle in 1970, he continued to write editorial pieces for mostly local newspapers. In 1972 he founded and published "The People's Yellow Pages" for Seattle and two years later founded the Seattle Sun community newspaper, in which he wrote a column. In the late 80's he wrote and delivered bi-weekly commentaries on NPR's local affiliate KPLU. In the 90's he mostly wrote and delivered insurance policies as an insurance broker.

His fictional pieces have been confined to his filing cabinet with an occasional story appearing in his Urban Politics email newsletter which he has published since 1996.
For a peek at them go to:
http://www.ci.seattle.wa.us/council/licata/up00dex.htm

"Princess Bianca and the Vandals" is his first novel. Having had dyslexia as a youth, he could not read until the age of nine. Consequently he has empathy for those struggling to read and wrote a novel for early readers.

The author can be contacted at
Nicholasjlicata@aol.com

THE ORIGIN OF
THE PRINCESS BIANCA TALE

The Princess Bianca tale traces its origin to Guangzhou, China, where the author's daughter lived for a year with her mother. During the year that she was gone, the author sent her tape recordings of the adventures of Princess Bianca. When huge demonstrations broke out in Guangzhou in connection with the Tiananmen pro-democracy movement in Beijing, she and her mother took flight from the city.

In their haste, the tapes along with other incidentals were left behind. The tapes were mistakenly mislabeled and shipped to a village in northern China. A camel trader who barely understood English found them several years later and took them for some unknown reason across the desert to the Mongolian Capitol of Ulaan Baatar.

The tapes remained in the backroom of a musty smoke shop in the middle of Mongolia for several more years, until a Seattle University professor stumbled across them while visiting Ulaan Baatar. He happened to stop by the shop to buy a pipe. One of the tapes was playing in the background and he recognized the author's voice from his radio commentaries. He bought the tapes and a pipe, and brought them back to Seattle.

Unfortunately the author had already rewritten the story several times by memory and no longer needed the tapes. They were recycled.

To order copies of "Princess Bianca & The Vandals" directly

from the publisher please send a check or money order for

$17.87

to:

Fratri Gracchi Publishing

705 2nd Ave. Suite 1100

Seattle, WA 98104

Please add $2.00 per book for postage and shipping.

WA State residents add 8.8% sales tax.

Make all checks payable to: Fratri Gracchi Publishing

To order Princess Bianca & The Vandals via credit or debit card,

visit the website:

http://www.princessbianca.org

The first 500 orders receive an author signed copy of the book!